D1524113

HEMLOCKS

A NOVEL

BEN SCHULZ

Copyright © 2021 Ben Schulz
All rights reserved
First Edition

PAGE PUBLISHING, INC.
Conneaut Lake, PA

First originally published by Page Publishing 2021

ISBN 978-1-6624-4424-1 (pbk)
ISBN 978-1-6624-4425-8 (digital)

Printed in the United States of America

CHAPTER 1

Jacob Abbott, aged twenty-two, had left Philadelphia early that very morning and, using several modes of transportation (ferry, donkey, another ferry, and walking seven miles), was aiming to make it home for supper. He was taller than his younger brother by three inches and stronger and had benefitted from more formal schooling. He learned from tutors up to age twelve, Aaron only to age ten—both brothers knew their arithmetic, logic, languages, and natural sciences—and Jacob even learned the fiddle. But it would be a mistake to call the Abbott boys "gentlemen." Both brothers were budding mechanics/ millers. This was respectable enough, and it guaranteed their place as "middling" in the socioeconomic stratosphere. It would certainly guarantee them employment, especially in the Jerseys. They knew a bit about agriculture, but their strengths lie in woodcraft and grinding grains. There would come a day they could own some land and maybe hire some help, but life no doubt would be a struggle.

A bachelor, Jacob had been engaged to be wed in 1773, but his bride-to-be died of consumption. Recently he was making this commute every few weeks, having landed steady work in the city. He knew the forks in the roads, the various groves of trees, the inns and taverns, and the dozens of small farms along his path. The moss-grown stones and handsome wooden doors, and lots of open land. It was forty-six miles, door-to-door.

It had been some weeks since the British had evacuated Boston, far to the chilly north, and Jacob would periodically question fellow travelers if any intelligence was known on the whereabout of His Majesty's fleet. It seemed nobody knew anything. Of course, he also had to stand guard against a possible attack from a drunken rebel; so far, his luck had been good. Although it often felt the Sons of Liberty were trolling the nearby woods, like wolves, and the eyes were on him, through the trees. But loyalism was dominant in Somerset and places south, but heading north, closer to New York, the cold clutch of loyalism thawed, and the warm passion of unapologetic rebellion increased. He walked and walked. And walked. At times he was joined above the head by quick flitting black bats. The smell of woodsmoke permeated from a nearby kitchen. Intelligence was wanting—His Majesty's fleet would land when they landed. Not before. So he walked.

*****

The magnificent constellation Leo, once again, was suspended high above New Jersey, and North America, and the planet, like an all-knowing power. A halo in the ink-black northern sky.

Leo belongs to the zodiac family of constellations. Twelve total. The Twelve Olympians are the principal gods of the pantheon, and what a special number. There are twelve. A dozen. For perhaps millions of years, Leo posed up there. And perhaps a million more.

"And that is the Regulus, which is his foreleg," the skinny seventeen-year-old said, lying in the grass on his back.

Aaron Abbott's two little sisters enjoyed his stories of the sky, for the stories featured a rich blend of drama, science, fact, and folklore. And if he got a scientific fact a tad incorrect, it wasn't the end of the world. Not here. They also liked to tug on his brown hair, fiddle with his waistcoat buttons, and poke him with their hoop stick. He was good company.

"And that is Jupiter. The lion is jumping over Jupiter. Do you see how he is angled?"

"Splendid."

"No, right there. There!"

"Oh yes."

Aaron looked up as he spoke, admiring this vast visual aid. It was a black, gorgeous evening in May. A cool wind blew through the yard, and every now and then an apple would thump down nearby. And a chicken would sometimes squawk over at the coop. There

4

was something regal about it, like a bold tapestry in ancient times. Staring at you, down at you; you cannot critique or mock me...

"Jumping over Jupiter. Both beginning with Js," the sister observed.

"That's right."

A moment later, the back door swung open; it was mother.

"Time for bed, little stargazers. Church tomorrow."

"But mother..." Charlotte and Eliza countered.

"No discussion—it is one of Father Henderson's last sermons before he sails for England."

The sisters give a nod of acquiescence. During this brief exchange, Aaron didn't move, still studying Leo, jumping over Jupiter. *Think about the ancient Greeks seeing this, and King Arthur, and Shakespeare, and our father fifteen years ago. Rest in Peace, Thomas Abbott. American-born and settled this property*, Aaron had to think...*1746 or 48.*

The door shut. "Aaron, why is Father Henderson sailing for England?" sister asked.

"He thinks the troubles with the rebels may worsen, and they may, he thinks, even come to Somerset County."

"Do you think so?" they asked their brother.

"Of course not. The troubles are Massachusetts troubles, maybe Connecticut. We are safe down here."

"Do you know where Connecticut is?"

"Yes, brother."

"Good. Far from here, thank God."

But big brother knew better. After a pause, he continued.

"Anyway, some gentlemen want to cross the ocean and be closer to London until this all passes over. Probably the wise course of action."

"Are we going to London?" the sisters wondered aloud. They are no longer interested in the sky but focused on Aaron (who was still fixated on Leo.)

"No, we are safe here in the Jerseys. Father Henderson will soon be back. You have friends right here and your school. This is our home."

Charlotte, the elder, says, "My teacher says the British Army will attack New York, and when they fight there, the rebels will come to New Jersey, and they will fight here. In the Jerseys!"

Aaron spoke up. "Let us not think about that right now. Do you see his front shoulder? Do you see his tail? I love that tail."

"Yes, Aaron," they said.

"Now, go inside and get some sleep."

"Yes, Aaron."

The door opened and then shut. Aaron, left alone, thought that Charlotte's teacher probably had it exactly right. Hopefully, however, the British could end the war in New York, and the Jerseys could be spared. Regal, powerful, majestic. Leo was the British empire, and they will pounce and crush their victim.

*****

Aaron stepped inside the Abbott house, in Somerset County, New Jersey. Mother wiped the sisters' mouths with her apron. It was a nice home: one full story with garret, sturdy pine floorboards, the walls whitewashed over lathe, and a reliable cypress roof. But the hallmark was the enormous fireplace, large enough for the young ones to walk in and out of, when not lit. During the winter, the family slid the dining table quite close to its warm glow. A long rifle hung over the fireplace, which used to belong to their deceased father. It was seldom used, except by the oldest boy Jacob. The interior was spartan and always clean—a few pewter dishes here, the family Bible and other books there. The old beams had absorbed decades of fragrance that included sea salt and damp leaves. Crooked old nails and tiny wooden posts jutted out of the beams. A portrait of Aaron's grandfather hung on the wall—he emigrated to the New World in 1717. Arthur Abbott, a hardworking farmer, found success with a number of crops: beans, squash, corn, peas, pumpkins, and peppers.

The sisters sauntered upstairs.

"Is Jacob to attend church tomorrow, Mother?" Aaron asked.

"I think not. He's still in Philadelphia working for the Robertsons."

Aaron took a sip of cold tea and faced his mother, choosing his words carefully.

"Do you deem it…safe, for us, to go to this Tory service?"

"Don't say that word!" Ms. Abbot cried.

"Sorry. Do you? For Eliza and Charlotte's sake?"

Mother didn't answer.

"The Sons of Liberty are a force. They have stretched their hand down here, at Somerset. Lord knows the reasons. We are—after all—a band of peaceful farmers. Still—we cannot deny, the rascals have been emboldened, Mother."

"Then the Lord will help us. Besides, we shall confuse your sisters if we forgo the service and timidly sit at home, with doors locked, living in fear. Your father would never allow that."

"Understood, Mother, but maybe we should retreat to the country for a few—"

Ms. Abbott cut him off. "Enough, Aaron. Off to bed. The situation is not yet too dire. God save the king."

"God save the king. Good night, Mother."

*****

That night a soft wind tapped intermittently along the thin panes. About fifty miles to the east, the contours of the land turned deeply rutted, and some of the oldest rocks in New Jersey (a mix of Precambrian granites and lower Paleozoic clastic and carbonate) threw up steep hills and small mountains, before suddenly all dropping off into the endless dark green ocean. There were wharves and docks and fishing vessels, busy all night but strangely quiet; and Perth Amboy and the lighthouse, where more Tory sloops and jon boats silently pushed off into the blackness, en route to Canada or England or other safe havens. The fish, oysters, crabs, mussels, none of them knew there was a war going on, and for a year at that. The soft waves still crashed into the Jersey Shore like they always had done. Everybody, and everything, slept save for the mighty Leo, millions of miles above. Protector and predator.

The Tory service next day was crowded and merry. No one could tell a war was going on. Trinity Parish was an Anglican church about four miles from the Abbott home, an easy walk, especially in nice weather. Only on special occasions—Easter, weddings, Christmas day—would the middle-class family splurge on a rented carriage ride. Trinity was the heart and soul of the area: a meeting place, a place of worship, and a place to conduct business with townsfolk. Mr. and Mrs. Abbott were married here. The boys were baptized here. Two years ago, Jacob, Aaron, and about a dozen other locals volunteered for two weeks to paint the church a pristine white. It sparkled on this sunny day.

Father Henderson was a champion for Somerset: teacher, mentor, community leader, and voice of divine providence. He had been a minister ever since Aaron's father moved the family here during the French and Indian War; Aaron was then a small tot. Now in his middle fifties, with long gray hair, he spoke these days with wisdom and maturity and calm intelligence. "Aye," he said, "the Sons of Liberty were among them, but fear not—the Lord's care will blanket us. We have his word. We represent the king and God and Heaven, and England is here to protect us! Soon enough, the colonies will calm their fiery spirits, and righteousness will prevail! We are England men. The Sons of Liberty will run its course and find other towns to threaten. Those misguided souls will soon see the light. My friends, we shall not fear. We shall embrace each other in this tumultuous year, 1776, in the Jerseys. We shall embrace our family, our community, and our detractors—because our detractors will see the light of our great eternal cause of balance and peace and order. God Bless the king of England. Forever!"

*****

Aaron, Charlotte, Eliza, and Ms. Abbott nodded and grasped each other's hands; and when it came time for hymnal, they bellowed out some soulful music, along with the two hundred others in attendance. Trinity was filled with hope and joy. Nearly everyone in congregation knew everyone else, and certainly all respected Henderson and his family. Aaron learned penmanship and the Scriptures from Henderson, during educational retreats at the parish as a boy. On two occasions, Aaron and Jacob and other boys visited New York City with Henderson as chaperone and saw *the* Trinity parish off

Wall Street. In fact, Henderson had known Reverend William Vesey. Henderson emphasized that "grace and honesty and charity" can atone for any past sins. Always take positive steps, no matter what past mistakes and disappointments. Aaron lived his life every day thinking about these things—grace and honesty and charity. Always.

Ms. Abbott took advantage of these gatherings: to worship, to socialize, to share recipe ideas with friends, to engage in some gossip, and to quickly reject possible suitors who were interested in her—that attractive forty-two-year-old smile and figure. She would have nothing of it. She loved her deceased husband, dead for about ten years now. (Henderson had sent her flowers and reminded her what the Bible said about grief and mourning...) She sat in her pew with focused confidence, shoulders back, pretty eyes and tight mouth, graying hair, youngish figure, sleek shoulders, and arms.

She looked fetching in a green-and-white floral print dress, cut low across the bosom, with a dark gray hat and black leather shoes. She had borne, in total, three boys and three girls, losing one baby girl to typhus and one baby boy to a mysterious illness. And a husband. There had been a time in the first years after his death that her face had drawn inward toward deepening lines. But now her cheeks had again softened and the old leather pouch of gold pieces, dating back to her father, was maintaining its weight as well. Jacob's industriousness was a blessing. Her two boys and two girls were marked success and a source of pride and happiness as was her fine home and colorful garden in Somerset. She was born in Somerset in 1734, and she had lived her entire life here; she had never traveled more than forty miles in any direction.

The family walked the four miles back home, on the exact path from five hours ago. Strangely, in so short a time, there were some differences that marked their path, unmistakable. Stark. Ms. Abbott tightened up and chose to ignore them, looking straight ahead. "Let's go."

The children, confused and surprised, in contrast, processed the new information and wrinkled their faces and thought; staring rather blankly on the trodden path. They were hand-painted signs, nailed to the trees. They spoke plainly enough.

One—ALL TORIES ARE SINNERS.

Another—"LOYAL" TO THE DEVIL. YOU ARE AN OBSTACLE.

And a third—**DEATH TO TORIES**

Were the signs terribly threatening? Perhaps. But still, the majority of Somerset citizens sided with the crown of England. Aaron's neighbors, friends, pastor, and family were with the seemingly safe, secure, and conservative majority, perhaps 80 percent to 20 percent "patriots." Probably the people behind these signs were not Somerset men, but coming down from New York.

Aaron read the signs and thought about where he was, two miles from home, a few paces off the New Brunswick Road, along the Trinity Path. Wildflowers, baby turtles down on the brook, fields of green corn stalks. He and his father rode together in these fields, and they told stories and they fished. Aaron remembered it all, as an eight-year-old boy. That field, that stream, the time they saw a skunk and his father whispered not to move an inch. The laughter, the tales, and the lessons. His father was a great man with a soul filled with adventure. And what would he say now? A man who sacrificed so much for the British empire (1756–58) at Fort Oswego and Louisbourg. A man who helped reestablish British excellence and might. The enemy was always France.

And what—who—is the enemy now? The answer was ourselves. Father's generation never would have let this slip. Our generation is losing it. These at one time were father's friends and associates. Remember?

All Tories are sinners. Death to Tories.

The Abbott family supped peacefully that evening, on soups and leftover cold meats, with warm pies straight from the hearth. It had been an invigorating and sunny day—seeing friends and neighbors at Trinity, running some light errands and chores, and sitting down to a late meal by lamplight. Aaron usually told his sisters stories while the matron of the house had a serious look about her. Always preparing, cooking, cleaning, straightening up. He was planning on reading a story aloud from the King James Bible for the sisters before bed, while Mother would clean up. He liked to point out that Ezra was a descendant of Aaron in the Bible and lived in exile in Babylon. The sisters would usually press their brother to tell the story of Balaam and the talking donkey. Many Sundays, they would have friends and neighbors over for an evening meal, but tonight it was only them.

"This is quite delicious, Mother," he said.

"Such a kind young boy! Yes, the raspberries are ripe. The bread came out nicely."

"Yes, Mother," the girls said.

"Hopefully those bunnies don't rip off the carrots we planted. We need to finish that little wooden fence. Sooner the better."

"Yes, Mother."

"Can we have pie after dinner?"

"No, you've had enough sweets for one day."

"Yes, Mother."

"Do we have any of those molasses cookies left?" Aaron asked.

"No, you ate them all," his mother answered.

"My teacher says George Washington doesn't truly believe in the rebellion, and he will soon give up."

"Quite right, quite right."

"Where does George Washington live, Aaron?"

"Somewhere in Virginia. Hot and swampy country. Glad it's not us!"

"Virginia?"

"Yes, most Southern men are a bit backwards in their thinking. Aaron asserted. Compared to us northerners, they are pretty stupid."

"Makes perfect sense to me," said Mother. "Why would a Virginia planter get mixed up in New England's business? Soon he will see those men for what they are."

"What's that, Mother?"

"A batch of fire ants."

"Fire ants!" The kids chuckled.

"What else does your teacher say, Eliza?" Aaron asked.

"She says George Washington and his Army have a good chance—because he is fighting on his native land. And the British Army is wholly unfamiliar…"

The mother said, "Rubbish! This is our native land. British since 1607!"

"Good point, Mother. The so-called patriots are misguided, misinformed, and mistaken! Washington knows nothing of New York and New England. Rubbish."

"Yes, Aaron."

"I would remind your teacher, all due respect, this land is British, through and through. Money, schools, government, tax codes, the church, the streets, the courts. What have the Americans done? Nothing."

"Good points, son. Eat your berries, stargazers," Mother said.

"Charlotte, sit up straight."

"Eliza, you know that's not how you hold your fork."

"Yes, Mother."

"That's how one of those Southern men hold their fork," Aaron joked. They giggled.

"Say, did you notice how beautiful the church was today in the sunlight. How white it was?"

"Here he goes again, telling us he painted it two years ago," sighed Charlotte.

"Aye. I painted the church two years ago!' Aaron bragged. "With Jacob too. I was on a ladder that must have been forty feet tall! We took turns holding the ladder. They paid us handsomely for that job, if I remember."

Outside, the crickets and small critters bellowed out a chorus of melodic verse, and like the tide of the ocean it seemingly never abated. It was getting late, nearly nine of the clock. The bright moon crawled across the black sky like a lonely skiff on the treacherous sea. It was quite windy; every now and again, a tree branch slapped against the back of the kitchen.

Mother cut her meat into small squares and barked out a comment to her youngest, "Eliza, what is that stain upon your shift?"

As Eliza looked down at this mysterious discoloration, the sounds of running feet came straight to the house: thumping, beating. The door swung open. It was Jacob—pale, weary, with an animated look.

The sisters were happy to see him, but Aaron and Mother could see in the man's eyes something was terribly wrong. "Jacob?"

"The devil has struck. Lord help us!" Jacob punched down hard on the table.

"Jacob?" they called out again.

"Are you hurt, brother?"

Aaron bolted from his seat and expected the worst. "Brother?" They all took a few cautious steps toward the strapping, exhausted man. Jacob gathered himself and prepared to speak.

"The damned rebels killed Father Henderson this night."

"Oh!" they mourned.

"Killed him dead. And they have set fire to Trinity."

"Oh Jacob!" Mother turned pale and wandered about her kitchen like a mad lady. Aaron bowed his head in despair. The little sisters cried quietly.

"Girls, go to your room!" Mother cried.

Aaron stepped to the window and gazed out dumbly, in the direction of Trinity. Jacob, face flushed, paced the room and constantly motioned with his hands.

"Oh Jacob," sighed Mother.

"Damned Sons of Liberty. Father Henderson did nothing to them," said Aaron. "Did you see anyone else?"

"Pratt was out there on the post road. He relayed the news."

"Damned rascals."

"They have brought the war to us," Jacob sighed.

"War in New Jersey? Unconscionable."

"Perhaps an isolated incident, brother. People want peace here. This is Somerset! Not fiery Harvard Yard!"

Jacob chuckled darkly. "Tell me the bloody difference, will ye. I've been a long time in Philadelphia. We Tories are in the minority, getting pushed out. Many have left. Everybody up and down the street has their own damn copy of that *common sense* rubbish. The changes are upon us. It's spreading! They say revolution, and I am seeing revolution…"

"Oh Jacob," said Mother.

"They are coming, brother. They are here. Mother, we are in the wrong place at the wrong bloody time. And you are either with them, or against them!"

13

Both girls hovered at the top of the stairs in the dark, looking down and listening in. Their eyes were shiny with fresh tears.

"Wrong place at the wrong time," Aaron repeated in a whisper.

Jacob marched over to the fireplace, grabbed the gun from the wall, and looked at his mother. "They will soon be sorry, coming to Somerset." It was a smoothbore Brown Bess musket, weighing about ten pounds, and it was about ten years old, a gift from an uncle. Jacob, face clenched, held it steady like a real combatant.

"Oh boys." Mother sighed. She looked out the window, slightly trembling.

"Lord help us," Aaron said.

CHAPTER 2

The colonies that July declared their "independence," and throughout the autumn, the British redcoats whipped George Washington's Army in a series of battles in and around New York. The country was in turmoil, and poor loyalists were in grave danger. Churches, storehouses, and farms were being destroyed throughout the mid-Atlantic by both forces. Smallpox was rampant. Three of their neighbors in fact were rocked by high fevers and chills, severe body aches, a twisted stomach, and a disgusting rash. A Somerset doctor explained that the smallpox pustules ran together into a single pus-filled rash that seeped, cracked, and had to be removed in large sheets. The future was far from certain.

The future of the Abbott family was also uncertain, although it was clear that they simply could not safely stick together. Since the violent death of their beloved minister in May, the entire county was in a stupor. Several families managed to escape to Canada; some tried to relocate to Fort Pitt or Hagerstown on the fringes of civilization. Many were cashing out their chips, folding everything up, and heading out to sea, England-bound. There were a few cases of loyalists caught in Somerset and put in prison, near Princeton College. New Jersey supplied the rebel armies with hundreds of brave lads with the taste of liberty on their lips. But hundreds more took up arms and fought for England. Aaron and Jacob did just this, like their father against the cursed French in 1757—because England was mighty and majestic, well-equipped and impeccably in order, with an undeniably grand legacy, which included William I, Henry V, Cromwell, Marlboro, Forbes, Amherst, and a Navy second to none. Aaron and Jacob would don the red fabric and march to glorious victory!

Their family, however, would not be witness to this. After much discussion and much gathering (and borrowing) of capital, Mother would depart with Eliza and Charlotte, and relocate to England. It was not an easy decision, but ultimately Ms. Abbott would call the shots. The conversations over several days went like this:

"The ocean crossing is dangerous, Mother!"

"Remaining in Somerset, surrounded by these cursed bandits, is dangerous," she countered.

"You have not enough food and medicine on your persons!"

"We will help each other on the voyage. We will band together."

"There are pirates and rebels. And bloody Spanish! What of those?"

"There are also British ships, our friends. British protection!"

"You can make new friends here. We can invest in a new region. This is the New World. We've accomplished so much in America!"

"Many of my dear friends have gone and I shall follow them. It's best for your sisters."

"Will you write us often?" Aaron asked.

"Of course, dears."

"Will you find a good school for the sisters?"

"Of course, dears. Remember I have been their mother for fourteen years!"

"Fair point." They both sighed.

"I am proud of you serving the king. Handsome boys. This war will be over soon enough. And we will be reunited, the Lord's will be done."

"We will be reunited," Aaron said.

*****

The *HMS Pursue* lay at anchor. Free Blacks, Germans, Dutch, random seamen, families in a frenzy, and other disreputable persons (thieves, prostitutes, hucksters) crowded all up and down the dark wharves. People were selling Bibles and snacks and blankets and doses of opium and mercury tablets. Some people were shouting they had newspapers. A cold wind was blowing, a great night to set sail. Aaron looked around with paranoia at the nefarious characters lurking in and out of the shadows. Were they spies? Thieves? Did they sabotage the ship? They sat and looked at Aaron, motionless, and eerily confident, almost grinning; in the dark mostly their silhouettes only stood out. They were like rats, stooping and waiting, under cover. They had eyes. They had motives, perhaps? Aaron looked at the little rat faces, in the shadows, and then to his surprise one of the characters stood up, adjusted himself, and began walking out of the shadows, under the light, slowly, toward the Abbot family. He had a wooden leg and walked with a limp, a hideously ugly face with a devilish grin. Slowly, slowly he got closer.

Jacob stepped forward. "Can I assist you, friend?"

"Might you have change if I gave you one shilling? Say, twelve pence if you will?" he spoke in a thick brogue, almost Scottish in flavor. Jacob smiled. He inspected the shilling carefully.

"This is a counterfeit. Bugger off, rat." The man made a frown and hobbled away.

"I will miss you terribly, Aaron," said Eliza, now twelve. Tears ran down her cheeks.

"I love you, sister." Aaron smiled and swallowed his sadness; he looked optimistic and handsome just then.

"I love you, Aaron."

"We will be reunited," repeated Aaron.

ALL ABOARD! A man bellowed from the gangplank.

That winter and spring, the Abbott boys joined the ranks of the British forces and began their training. The deep association with Somerset was forever severed. Their days now were filled with marching, drill, training, cleaning, eating, and more drill, marching, and cleaning. They cleaned their guns, they wiped down and buffed the cannon, they ran errands, they helped feed the horses, and they took turns on picket and security duty. Always they set down low in rank underneath native Britons, who felt themselves much more superior. Tories from Jersey were linked closer to American patriots, and from the British perspective they must be kept an eye on, pushed, harassed, managed, all the time. Without let up. Until victory. Tories, although fighting with the right side, were second-class citizens, plain and simple.

Jacob was trained in artillery, loading, and firing cannon, the transport of shot and shell. And Aaron—smaller, skinnier, a step behind—was given a job as courier and runner. He would run around camps and tents and barns in northern Jersey, but come September 1777, when the British took Philadelphia, Aaron delivered up and down pretty city blocks within this, the brainchild of William Penn.

Some would say the British were bumbling and wasting time. They had massive advantages over the colonials: numbers, military expertise, naval power, prestige and pluck, and supreme arrogance up and down the ranks. Of course, they had an established government with deep pockets. And yet the war continued. King George and his advisers had selected William Howe, born in 1729 who had served under General Wolfe at Quebec back when the Abbott boys were learning to count and chew their food. Howe was a great leader, and his armies did brilliantly in New York, winning again and again and again. He could win. But could he win…the war?

But Howe, for all his faults, seemed to be in control. About nine thousand confident and tested British troops manned the Germantown camp, with about three thousand held in reserve in the city below. A possible American attack was talked about, but its likelihood was doubtful; pretty soon the weather would turn and both armies would need to find a winter camp. Philadelphia was a coveted prize that would not be given up easily.

Jacob and several dozen loyalists attached themselves to the British Fourth Brigade and, in late September, encamped along Old York Road, about eight miles above Philadelphia. They were surrounded by large wheat fields, stone mills, fresh streams, and good dry roads. There were fresh-hewn wood fences stretching along both sides of the road. The men safeguarded their cannon inside a large barn with a gambrel roof, and Jacob was tasked with keeping the wheels greased and applying a daily polish to its bronze barrels. A Latin inscription was carved into the barrel with presumably some motto of inspiration, but most of the rank and file knew not its translation. They also inventoried ammunition for the side boxes, mostly case shot and round shot. His superior officer was a young captain named Murray. The overall commander of the outfit was General

Agnew, but Jacob never once saw the man. And Agnew of course reported to Howe, who headquartered a couple miles in the rear.

It was October 4. Early-morning fog blanketed the countryside. Jacob and his unit heard distant firing far to the left, near the Benjamin Chew House. Plumes of smoke filled the air and mixed with the clouds. The clanging and popping noises increased in intensity. Men and horses began to stir. The battle had begun. The rebels, fresh off the loss at Brandywine, were nothing if not determined. Captain Murray dashed back and forth and barked orders, readying his men for a possible assault. To Jacob's left, the British cannon pumped out some deafening booms almost unceasingly. The sun had risen slightly higher. He could hear men yelling, and after a short time, he saw his first battle casualty. A boy was shot through the stomach and shoulder and he collapsed, and with a look of casual surprise on his face he attempted to quell the bleeding with both his hands. Jacob continued to watch the boy suffer. He turned in the dirt and then turned the other way; his knees jerked up and then fell back, and then he stopped moving forever.

The Battle of Germantown would shift slightly toward Jacob's front. Americans under General Greene and General Stephen came pouring across the fields with their navy-blue coats and cream-colored pants—many hundreds of them. Virginia Continentals under Peter Muhlenberg fought vigorously, pushing deep into the British lines. The Americans ran proudly across the fields, with flag bearers and drummer boys in tow. These lads approached Old York Road.

Captain Murray was a good soldier, and he stayed calm, organizing a counterattack. The Virginians met several of Jacob's comrades, and both would fight with the bayonet in some brutal close-range fighting. Jacob helped maneuver the cannon and pass the boxes of ammo, crouching low, following orders. His eyes were wide, his mouth shut tight, his arms working fast, and every so often his head ducking with each crashing sound in his vicinity. Pump, reload, ignite, fire. Pump, reload, ignite, fire.

Sharp fragments of surrounding fences tore apart seemingly every few seconds. The rhythmic banging was terrible. Men next to Jacob dropped in pain, having caught the sharpshooter's bullet. Many

American bluecoats, just ahead in the fields, dropped at a higher rate. The engagement looked favorable for the British. It looked as though the British troops maintained a stronghold on the Chew House, and the Americans were forced backward. It was hard to see with all the smoke, but the banging sounds were beginning to fade. One of the mighty steeds next to Jacob was shot through the neck and killed. Pump, reload, ignite, fire. Pump, reload, ignite, fire. Murray did not let up his assault.

Jacob had little doubt of the battle's outcome, for he had a British heart, with British pride, and supreme confidence in combat; his entire unit did. The Americans, although they slightly outnumbered the redcoats, simply could not win. That was the mindset and that was a part of the rigorous training. The Americans cannot win. The Americans lost all their battles, and that was not about to change. Jacob felt his pride swell with each blue-coated rebel fall dead in the grass, his rifle dropped next to him. He hoped one of these could be Greene, or maybe even Washington, the most treacherous rebel of the lot.

Captain Murray and some of Jacob's regiment charged ahead and captured many of Greene's men. Just after midday, Jacob felt the sting of a bullet graze his left bicep; he faltered to the ground, his hat falling off, and his head knocked into the wheel of the cannon. But the wound was only slight, and he would be back on his feet within seconds. The adrenaline pumped through his body, and he felt for the first time like a British soldier. The Americans cannot win. Pump, reload, ignite, fire.

He began to see the Americans' backs, as most turned and jogged back the way they came. Some hobbled, some sprinted, some crawled. Many took shelter behind Lucan's Mill. An American flag lay tattered in the grass. Several dead and wounded men, mostly Americans, were strewn across the field. Jacob's unit at last silenced their firing; their cannon sat and cooled as the sun sank lower and almost all Americans had fled. There was a drum laying on the field, cream and brown, that a few British boys snatched and called their own. They ran past the eleven-year-old drummer boy, the American, dead like a stone, bullet holes in his back and shoulder.

In the early evening, Jacob got his wound dressed, and he had a brief conversation with the unit medic. All seemed right. When he stepped out of the medical tent, he saw an orderly row of American prisoners marching directly next to the tent. Their faces were smudged, and their eyes stared straight south; some of their shoes were coming apart. They marched. Dozens and dozens and dozens passed. Many young men from Virginia, Maryland, New Jersey. Thin and determined, but exhausted. About 240 marched by. Many were only 16 or 17 years old, younger even than Aaron, and Aaron was of course a young and inexperienced lad.

"Still think you have a chance, rebels?" a man shouted.

"You chose your fate, boys…" British officers chuckled. "You chose your fate."

Jacob asked the man next to him, "Where are they taking them?"

"To Philadelphia" was the reply. "And then, to hell."

With the battle won, Howe's possession of Philadelphia remained secure. The sky turned black, and the moon suspended itself over the field, where dozens of bloodied and moaning Americans struggled in the grass. Jacob was looking forward to going back to the city to reconnect with Aaron; doubtless the latter heard all about the battle and was concerned about his big brother's well-being. Some of the British walked down Germantown Road, drinking from canteens. They relayed the startling news that General James Agnew had been killed in battle by one of the damn rebel marksmen.

And the Mohawk Indians crossed the road up ahead, dressed in highly decorated moccasins, and their necks were festooned with metal jewelry, partially shaved heads. They walked tall and straight, holding knives and guns at their side. Almost all the Mohawk people allied with the British; they had a deep relationship going back decades and together wanted the colonials to be beaten.

The rest of the year, 1777, during the cold weeks, with no combat on the horizon, most boys like Jacob were relegated to menial jobs—they cleaned jail cells, split wood, cooked and served on ships, etc. It smelled like vinegar and sweat down in the hold, so the men would tie kerchiefs across their mouths, or else they would vomit. The November air turned chilly and raw. The days, although shorter, were filled with marching, patrol, cleaning weapons, and attending little lectures and sermons. Corn, wheat, rye, and squash had been harvested and was in abundant supply all over town.

Jacob would meet Aaron occasionally for a nice meal. One of the popular hangouts was the Robert Dudley Tavern on Market Street. It had a huge dining room, a fully staffed kitchen, and in the rear a beer garden lined with colorful flowers and potted shrubs.

Jacob cut aggressively with his fork and knife. "Better than that bloody cornmeal gruel, huh?"

"Aye, brother," said Aaron.

"Eat some more fish!" he barked to his brother and drank from his metal cup. "It's fresh!"

"Thank you," Aaron replied.

"Did you send that letter to mother and sisters?" Jacob asked, chewing his food.

"Yes, last evening," Aaron said.

"Well done. Our man of letters!"

"Aye."

"Tonight, I am going to find a gambling table, throw everything I have toward it, and make a goddamn fortune. Ha!"

"I have to work tomorrow." Aaron sighed.

"Hey, you have a smoke?"

The boys sat among their empty plates, leaned back, and enjoyed their pipes.

Aaron said, "One of the boys on my route says the French will join the war. It will be just like 1758 again!"

Jacob said, "And just like 1758, we kill them bastards. The French are a bunch of whores. They don't have the Sun King any longer. They are done!"

"Quite right."

"Yesterday's news."

"Quite right."

Their plates and bowls were cleared away. "So what have you been doing, brother?"

"I bought a telescope from an artisan in town."

"Is Leo still up there?" Jacob joked.

"Yes, sir, every night."

"You and your damn stars…ha… Hey, doll! More New England rum and spruce beer over here!" Jacob hollered.

"Yes, handsome," she said.

Aaron leaned in. "I have to hand it to you. You fought in a battle! Cannot believe it." Aaron sighed. "Just like Father!"

"Aye. It's an experience I hope you never have to see. Seeing that struggle. The fight. The death. Boys and young men…"

Aaron: "When we win this war, they'll make a statue of you in Somerset. Eh, brother?"

"We'll see, brother. War's not over."

Somebody in Jacob's unit walked in, bent down, and spoke loudly in Jacob's ear: "They are playing whist tonight at Clarkes. Won't you go?"

"Yes, will clean them out. Feeling lucky." The man slapped Jacob on the shoulder and walked away. "Can I borrow a little brother?" His drinks were delivered.

"Cheers, Dolly."

"Yes, handsome."

Jacob: "The British can be assholes, but hey, we get paid fairly well! Cheers."

"Cheers," said Aaron. Aaron gave him two shillings. "Here."

"Splendid! You'll get it back, and then some."

Aaron drank his tea and Jacob slammed his rum. "Here's to killing Washington's Army!"

They laughed. Other British men and women cheer also. "Degenerates!"

Jacob, visibly drunk, stood up quickly. "Let us go find that whist table. C'mon. I'm feeling lucky."

And deep into the night, like all good soldiers do (on a night off) they played whist and other games of chance, they drank some New England rum and spruce beer, and they partied, and Jacob forcibly kissed a married barmaid and was slapped across the face, until they were kicked out and told to go home.

Life went on. Aaron was a courier, and Jacob was getting his arm repaired, good as new. Aaron got a lot of exercise for the next few weeks, crisscrossing city blocks with his bundles of mail, delivering all over the north end of town. Military dispatches, mostly. Requirements to the citizens regarding military ordinance, British regulations, curfews. He bunked with other errand boys and aides in the neighborhood of Fishtown, while his older brother camped with thousands of troops across the river in Camden.

Because of his recent injury in combat, Jacob was relegated to prison duty, just outside the city, until his arm could fully heal. There were about 5 loyalist troops working in shifts, to keep an eye on the penned up colonial troops. There were about 250, but on Jacob's block there were 27. Many of them were merely lads—16 or 17, younger even than Aaron. They were from all over but mostly from Delaware and New York. Jacob would mop and stroll the halls, and mop some more, occasionally direct the Negro hands—which bedpan needed removing or who needed water. But mostly he just sat, as a sort of security.

He did this every day, faithfully, like a soldier. Most days he reported to work at 10:00 a.m. and worked until 9:00 p.m., or whenever his replacement came. He would stroll and mop and clean and keep the area secure. When he was on his rounds, he noticed that no matter what time of day or what the circumstance, inside one particular cell there was always, constantly—every time—a sixteen-year-old Maryland boy sitting and staring at him. Many others were dozing, or on the toilet, or making something with their industrious dirty fingers. But not this boy. He sat and stared at Jacob, mouth closed, shoulders back, like a man stuck in a painting. Staring. Jacob walked and watched, walked and watched, and was constantly annoyed by this. After eight days, he had enough.

"What are you *looking* at?" Jacob called out.

The boy said nothing, nor did he flinch. Their eyes locked as if that was God's plan.

"What is it?" Jacob hollered.

"Are you dumb, boy? Huh?" No response.

Jacob would mop, stroll, sit, stroll, and then mop. His block was always clean. He was content in his not-so-exciting position, save for that boy. Their eyes locked. Again. Again. Like a beam of light that enters a room.

"What are you *looking* at?" Jacob called out. "Chrissakes."

Aaron updated his journal: *Went to the library—November 23, '77. I checked out Tobias Smollett's novel The Adventures of Roderick Random.*

It was considered bawdy and earthy, and Aaron loved it. He befriended a wheelwright named Ross. He read John Campbell's *Lives of the British Admirals.* He continued to create tools and trinkets out of bone and antler. He read the *London Magazine.* Unlike his brother, he enjoyed Philadelphia. It was so cosmopolitan—the Europeans, the aristocrats, the Jews, the artists, and the businesspeople. He and Ross would go fishing together, go to the library, and frequent some of the coffee houses along Arch Street and Church Street.

They went to some services at the Quaker meeting house. Aaron read the Bible for an hour every night.

And then he wrote another letter to his sisters and mother. He did not go into full detail about the recent battle, and Jacob's injury, and the perpetual social unrest in the city, lest he worry them. He read his books. He turned nineteen. He was skinny, healthy. Optimistic. Christmas 1777 was approaching.

The five-foot-eight, 131-pound courier worked hard, six days a week. There was a spring in his step. Unlike the other boys working their routes, he didn't drink or take any opiates. His main vices were simply dark tea and sweet pipe tobacco.

*****

One night, Aaron and Ross were walking back through the city after a long afternoon of fishing. They were talking about the birch and pine, how enormous they were near the shoreline. And they strolled back under the street lanterns. It was quite late.

And then two prostitutes stepped out of the shadows and began walking with the boys. "Evening, soldiers! Handsome men, aren't they?"

"Wow, handsome men they are!"

"Good evening, ladies." Ross was excited, flirtatious. Aaron was nervous. The ladies were close to thirty, not remarkably attractive, but they had a sparkle to them, like they were performers.

Ross whispered to Aaron, "Say, you got any money?"

"What?" Aaron asked incredulously. "These are dirty women. They carry diseases."

"Soldiers, only eight livres for some fun. Great fun!"

"You deserve a little fun!" they said. The four of them walked for a bit, slowly.

"Do you want to get your pecker hard, soldier?"

"On a cold night as this, you deserve to keep that pecker warm…"

Ross apparently was interested in great fun; he immediately put his arm around one of the ladies. They talked and laughed. Aaron continued walking.

"Soldier, how about you?" she said to the young courier.

"No, thank you," said Aaron. His companion was wearing an outrageous white wig and silk hat, donned in an old violet dress. She smelled like cheap oils and stale smoke.

"Perhaps, if not sensual pleasure—I can interest you in… information."

"What?" he asked, stopped in the street.

"Are you a learned man?" she asked, getting close to his cheek.

"Sure. Had the best tutors in the Jerseys!" he said, partially joking; and as he said this, he looked for Ross, but unfortunately, that man and his new date were clicking away over the cobblestones.

"Ask me any question in the world, anything you can think of, and if I answer correctly, you pay me eight livres. Deal?"

Aaron looked at her like she was from another planet. "Any question in the world?"

"Anything. I will answer!"

"Mighty confident, are ye."

"Aye, soldier."

Aaron thought for a while. He shifted his feet and then he smiled. "Are you familiar with *Gulliver's Travels?*"

"Um hmm," she said.

"Aye. Tell me, lady, the actual title of Swift's work. The full title!"

She said, "*Travels into Several Remote Nations of the World. In Four Parts. By Lemuel Gulliver, First a Surgeon, and then a Captain of Several Ships.*"

26

"Damn impressive. Here's your money." Aaron was understandably flabbergasted.

"Thank you." She looked at the money.

"You should be a librarian." Aaron said.

"I'm saving up to engage a tutor…"

"Right," Aaron said dismissively. "Pleasure to meet you."

Aaron began to leave, but the young lady said, unexpectedly, "I can also predict the future."

"You can predict the future? A lady in your profession?"

She gave him a look.

"I didn't mean it like that…" he said. "And you want to get paid for this too I suppose?"

"No. this one is pro bono." A pause. "You will not stay here," she said.

"What?"

"You will be leaving soon. Yes, soon." Her voice changed slightly, a faux fortune teller. She squinted her eyes and tapped her chin with her finger, like a deep thinker.

"Where?" asked Aaron, playing along.

"In the forest. I see the forests, soldier. Away from the ocean. You are nearly eaten by a bear! You want to run away from him, you do. But the bear will—"

"The bear will?" Aaron asked sarcastically.

"Control the situation, completely." She playfully roared like an animal and laughed. Then she turned and walked down the street.

He watched her walk and thought to himself, *Crazy bat. She's heard too many wild tales…*

He went home, alone. He noticed *Gulliver's Travels* sitting on his corner desk. Well, he will never see that eight livres again. Sigh.

Another December day in the city but I cannot say a Merry one, he wrote in his journal.

He blew out his candle and slept.

CHAPTER 3

Philadelphia had changed dramatically in the months since the British took it over. The market days—chickens, fruits, hogs, pumpkins, squash and the rest, and the bartering and hollering—were subdued. The coffee houses were no longer filled with engaged locals and boys hawking newspapers but, rather, arrogant British military men. On their off days, they sat and smoked, playing backgammon, cribbage, or whist. Many storefronts were closed up. The once-bustling wharves were now heavily regulated and mostly quiet. The custom-house officers in town resembled more military police and armed security. This was war.

But the streets were still straight and the many homes still elegant. The Schuylkill still flowed majestically on the west, the Delaware River on the east—no British occupation could take that away.

Aaron, as courier, continued to deliver messages up and down Chestnut, Water, and Market Streets and Second, Third, and Fourth Streets and the rest. He walked past churches and schools and the poorhouse, the milliner and apothecary and theater, and the statehouse. Occasionally he would deliver to the north side of town, along Vine Street, in the vicinity of some beautiful old homes.

That's where he met Jane.

It was an elegant urban mansion on Vine Street built around 1760. It had tough yellow pine floorboards with decorative oil cloth, Prussian blue wallpaper in the public spaces, and black walnut handrails leading up from the central passage.

There were six fireplaces. One of the larger parlors facing south featured a late Baroque style (1760) sofa with cabriole legs and restrained carvings. In the small parlor facing east, there was a Queen Anne-style card table, complete with ivory betting chips. Fancy-looking glasses adorned most every room on the ground floor, and the dining room had three whale-oil lamps.

Jane Canterbury, the same age—nineteen—as Aaron, grew up with an aunt and uncle in Delaware. When the war broke out, her uncle joined the American Continental Army in New York, and her aunt moved to Virginia. It was arranged for Jane to move in with her wealthy grandparents on Vine Street in the largest city in America, the urban brainchild of William Penn. Many locals fled the city in 1777, but Jane and her grandparents remained, pledging allegiance to the king and obeying every random and annoying stricture from the red-coated martial authority. For a woman of her station, Jane did not seek employment; she mostly stayed indoors and read her many books and wrote letters to her aunt. She did sometimes welcome suitors, as a number of eligible British soldiers would converse with her in the doorway, or through the parlor window, or at market. So far, as the Christmas holiday approached, none of these suitors were successful. Jane, who had blossomed into a lovely young woman, was unattached.

"Where do we keep the creamware dessert plates?" Jane asked the housemaid.

"The second cupboard, behind the knife box."

"Thank you, Molly."

"Make sure you leave enough of the great cake for your grand-mother. Last time you nearly ate the entire cake."

"Yes, Molly."

Jane took a healthy bite and sat contentedly. She stared at a newspaper next to her, which detailed General Burgoyne's surrender at Saratoga. The article speculated that France, and maybe Spain, would now enter the war against Great Britain.

"My heavens."

Molly spoke up as she was standing by the window. "There he is! That handsome young courier. I see him every week..."

"Who, Molly?"

"This dark-haired lad. He delivers the post for the major, I suspect. And does a fine job if I must say so. A fine job I tell ye."

"What is he—thirteen, fourteen? He's a child, I suspect," Jane joked.

But Molly corrected this notion. "Nothing of the sort! Twenty, I would guess. Handsome chap. Stands straight as a rod."

"Molly, get away from the window! He may see you," Jane said.

"Very well. But he shall see me, and you, at some time or another. This war will not end tomorrow. People need their mail!"

"For certain," Jane said as she read more about the Burgoyne story. Sixty-two hundred men captured as POWs! She set the paper down and took another bite of the great cake. "But if he's twenty, he probably has a wife."

Shoulders back, wavy brown hair, and with cute dimples, the attractive Jane took a big bite of cake and sat, chewing, sitting under a Dutch still life in an ostentatious frame. A Rachel Ruysch, perhaps 150 years old.

And Molly, early thirties, donned in white apron and her hair held up by a cloth cap—an immigrant from Ireland—dried the dishes and folded linens and, in the afternoon, swept the hallway clean.

*****

"What are you *looking* at, you turd! You runt!" Jacob screamed into the stank cell. But the Maryland boy snug in his room only sat and looked at Jacob. Unblinking.

A voice down the hall bellowed. "Scrub the latrine, American." Jacob rolled his eyes.

"Officer! Officer!"

"What is it, son?" Jacob answered.

"I think there is a dead man next to my cell."

Jacob dropped the mop handle and walked over, half-frustrated. He walked, the faces of the weak and scarred faces of the imprisoned growing ever larger. It smelled.

"What in the Lord…here? where the little turd sits? Jesus, that stench!" he grumbled.

It smelled something awful in the cell. Abbott covered his face with his brown scarf. Sure enough, Jacob leaned into the gate, and the sixteen-year-old boy was staring at him, as always. Other boys were in there, per usual, and there was a lump on one of the beds. A sleeping man?

"You there, Goldilocks. Is that man sleeping? Is he hurt? Go over there and poke him."

"I think he's dead, sir."

"Go poke him. Jesus, the smell. Do it! Now!" Jacob shouted through his scarf.

"Scrub the latrine, American!"

"Shut your bloody mouth!" Jacob yelled back.

They poked him, holding their nose. "I think he's dead, sir."

"Jesus." Jacob looked at the boy again. His face was turning red, his body stiffened.

"That dead man shows more life than you, little turd." He pressed his face against the cold bars. "What are you *looking* at, you turd! You runt!" Jacob screamed. "Goldilocks, what is up with this kid?"

"Private Tracey?"

"I guess so! Him!" Jacob pointed.

"He was captured at Fort Stanwix last summer, and tortured."

"Tortured?"

"Aye. By the Tuscarora peoples. Something brutal."

"What happened?" even though he was addressing the golden-haired soldier, Jacob's eyes were locked on this Private Tracey, and Tracey's on his.

"They burned both his feet, that's why he can't walk. And they stabbed his back with a dozen arrowheads. Finally, they cut out his damn tongue. He can't speak. And they left him there to die. But one of the British regiments found him, Tuchman's men, brought him here on a prisoner wagon."

"Goddamn savages…" Jacob swallowed, and looked at the poor lad. "Private Tracey…"

"Aye. Such is war. Man's sensibilities are dwarfed," he said.

"And how did you get in here, son?" Asked Jacob.

"Captured at Brandywine Creek, sir."

"Right. September. I was finishing up my training then."

"Aye. I think I got me a damn Brit before they took me in."

"I am glad. Did you ever see George Washington?"

"No, sir."

"Where you from?"

"Brooklyn, New York. And yourself?"

"None of your business," Jacob said half-jokingly.

"If Private Tracey here got his tongue cut out and cannot speak, how pray tell do you know his story?"

"He wrote it down for us on these pages." The Brooklyn man held out the little book. Jacob reached through and took the pages and scanned them quickly; it was just as depressing, maybe more so...

I was captured on August 17 by the Tuscarora Indians. They killed many of us, and women and children. They lit hot coals and cooked my feet very black. They stabbed me and poked me with arrowheads and then...

"Heavens... I can't read this. Take it." Jacob nodded to the Brooklyn man and walked away, his eyes fixed on Private Tracey. He walked twelve paces, and their eyes never left the other. Like a ghoulish portrait painting. For the next three hours Jacob scrubbed the latrine and mopped the floors.

He walked several more paces, turned a corner, and saluted.

"What is it?"

"I think there's a dead man in cell eight." Jacob said.

"Christ..."

The next day was bitterly cold. December winds kicked up along the Schuylkill. Trash barrels sometimes were knocked over by the natural force. Bird feeders swayed back and forth. Wooden signs on iron hooks also danced in the gusts. A small flurry of snow would spray the area, off and on; nothing stuck. Some people were putting out holly and wreaths and other holiday decor, and many chimneys were bellowing out hot, sweet, and dark smoke that smelled something fantastic. The streets and sidewalks were hard as hickory. Aaron was dressed in his warmest and most handsome attire: black cloak, thick vest, beige scarf, dark red woolen cap, and delivered mail to the customs house and bumped into Molly and Jane.

"I beg your pardon, sir. Could you direct us to Water Street? I have appeared to have gotten us lost again!" Molly said. Aaron stopped to address them, and he focused on Molly, because Molly's friend was so distractingly beautiful, that he could not make sustained eye contact. Her friend might have been fifteen, maybe older?

"Sure, madam. Water Street is behind you, three blocks. Do mind your step!" Aaron answered.

"Oh, lovely boy. Thank you."

"You're welcome." Aaron and Jane looked at each other. One second. Two seconds. Jane blinked quickly and looked off behind, at one of the taverns. She shuffled.

"You are wearing handsome shiny boots, sir," said Molly. "Are they commissioned by the Army?"

"*Molly*," interjected Jane, embarrassed.

"Thank you, Molly," Aaron said in a deep, confident voice. "They are my boots."

Molly smiled. "You know my name, and what pray tell is yours?"

"Aaron. Aaron Abbott. At your service..." He did a half bow and smiled, with an awkward but charming formality.

"A pleasure to meet you, handsome fellow. And this is Jane."

Aaron and Jane exchanged pleasantries. She had eyes like a goddess. She was about five foot five with a pleasant color in her cheeks. Aaron was starting to feel out of his element, and he wanted to break this off...when—

"Jane, stay here. I need to purchase some sugar," Molly called out and trotted off.

Aaron and Jane stood in the street and looked at each other for a few seconds, and then they uttered some terrible small talk that meant nothing. A man walked by with a large barrow holding a cage full of noisy chickens. Nearby, dogs were barking. The wind through town forced the young man to place a slight hold on his black cap.

"The holly looks nice," she said.

"Yes, it does," he said.

"Christmas is my favorite time of year," she said.

"Aye. Pretty wonderful."

A man danced by and handed them a bulletin for *The Recruiting Officer*. "Come see the show! The best in North America!" Then he gave another. "Come see the show! The best in North America! Come see the show! The best in North America!" He went on dancing and pitching the upcoming performance to all the people he encountered along the streets.

Jane took a step forward to Aaron. "I have not been to the theater in ages. I would like to go." She beamed.

"It's a joyous experience. According to my brother. Never been, myself," he admitted.

"Maybe I shall attend this—*Recruiting Officer*," Jane said, or rather—hinted.

"If it suits you. Great play! I read some of it last year, at the library." Aaron looked at his feet and thought of a way to break this off and continue with his afternoon. "It was a real pleasure, Ms. Jane, but I—"

"I know what. Would you like to attend *The Recruiting Officer* with me?" Jane said. She didn't seem nervous at all when she spoke but completely relaxed and gushing with a sincere smile.

"Go to the theater?" Aaron asked dumbly.

"Yes. Go to the theater." She blinked.

"Well, I don't know. I—I just met you." Flirting. This was surreal and stupendous; he had never been on a real date before. He had no experience with women. Those eyes. Of course, he had never been *asked out* before. That mouth, that figure. This woman was stunning, and she was interested is *his* company? His body felt nervously numb.

"I, uh. That would be…splendid. This Friday I am furloughed. We could—go to the show."

"You will go?" She smiled.

"I…yes, I will go." Aaron smiled nervously. "I will call on you at six of the clock. And your address?"

"Three eighty Vine Street, sir."

"Yes, that's on my delivery route."

"I wouldn't know," Jane fibbed.

"Call me Aaron."

"And call me Jane." She smiled; time stood still.

Aaron lifted his cap, did a quick bow, and quickly darted down a side street. The way she said "sir" to him made his heart hurt a little. His pulse quickened; he was cruising with hot confidence. Those green eyes, light-brown hair, smile, her voice! Good heavens.

"Come see the show! The best in North America!" the annoying thespian called out.

"You gave me one. I'll be there, friend," Aaron said coolly, holding up his brochure.

*****

The red-coated officer came down the stone steps, with two assistants at his back. The jingling of keys. The pop and clank of an unlocking sound. And they looked at the floors and the walls and the overall area, and they looked at Jacob Abbott. Jacob stood at attention.

The area was remarkably clean and bare, decluttered. A mop and bucket sat in the corner, smelling like soap. Jacob had a confident look on his face. His shoulders were back, and his chin jutted out, perpendicular to his smooth face.

The officer asked his assistants how many prisoners were in this corridor of the prison.

"Twenty-seven, sir."

"Twenty-seven. Quite right."

The man looked at the ceiling, the floors, and the bucket of clean soap; he circled back toward Jacob and stopped. He made a strange face.

"Do you smell that?"

"Do you smell that—it smells like piss."

Jacob didn't answer; he looked straight ahead. In fact, nobody answered.

He then shouted, "I need soldiers to keep these damn cells clean!" His face was beet red. And then he unbuttoned his pants and proceeded to urinate in one of the corners of the area. The urine hit the stone wall, and a tuft of steam rose up. A puddle formed at the officer's feet. He buttoned up his pants and turned.

"It smells like piss in here." One of the assistants chuckled, and then the other. The urinator smiled.

He walked right up to Jacob and said, "Do your duty." And he punched him right in the stomach. Jacob groaned and coughed, but after a few seconds he stood back at attention.

"You're Jersey dung, soldier. Jersey dung. After this war, you'll be blacking my boots." The man stared at Jacob for three or four seconds; all was silent.

"Yes, sir!" Jacob shouted.

"What's your name, man?" the officer barked.

"Abbott, sir."

"Well, Abbott, looks like you have some piss to clean up."

He made a motion to his cohorts, the keys were produced, the door flung open, and the three men walked quickly up the stone steps. Jacob walked over to his mop, stepping over the puddle. He held his stomach for a moment and grimaced.

*****

Aaron walked up and down the street with his bundles and packages, sometimes avoiding the boys and girls at their games of hoop and stick, and past the pretty storefronts downtown that were selling snuff and snuff boxes, tankards made of pewter, pocket watches, sterling silver, other gifts, and the always-crowded milliner. Closer to the port, it smelled more like pine tar and linseed oil and lumber. Wagon wheels rattled up and back on cobbled streets. The longshore crews passed crates and barrels, at a steady clip. All day men walked around with ropes and cables and tools. It was noisier and busier, and some of the ships were always a marvel to behold.

The Recruiting Officer play was a success, and so was a second meetup at a coffee house. Aaron was starting to recognize a wonderful fragrance that Jane had dabbed on her beautiful white neck.

And so they started dating. It was inevitable. Undeniable spark, the kids simply couldn't walk away from it or get it out of their heads. They went to the theater, they drank fragrant tea, they talked, they exchanged books to read, and after two more dates they even kissed.

Aaron began writing her letters. Every word and each sentence was precisely chosen, and Jane loved reading them. In sum, the first ten days' relationship was off to a white-hot start.

Aaron would get up early and, as was his custom, would shave with the aid of a looking glass. He had an extra spring to his step. Jane dominated his thoughts. He liked to wear his fancy wine-colored breeches. A young man shaves his face differently, while smitten with a beautiful girl who lives across town. There is vigor, purpose—careful not to cut yourself!

Some nights he and Jane would go to Smith's Tavern—seven shillings a head for dinner. They had pork, soup, cabbage, and beets. Good wine. Live music. Jane liked to sit by the cast-iron fireback and grate. It was toasty and intimate. Jane loved the fireplaces—the uniqueness, the character, the social aspect—and she was stunningly beautiful talking about Cervantes or Plutarch or the latest fashion trend she had read about from Paris.

Weeks went by, and their relationship got even stronger. The week of Christmas, there was an advertisement for the upcoming *The Miser*, by Moliere, slated for the spring. They also saw a poster for Henry IV in a theater on the other side of town.

"Oh Aaron, Shakespeare!"

"Never heard of him. Is he good?"

"Very funny. Can we go?"

"Of course, love." Aaron had no plan but not having a plan was his plan; he acted like a gentleman and caressed her elbow and kissed her and wrote her many letters. If they were going to see a Shakespeare play, then things were getting serious…

Molly was dusting the mantelpiece and picking up tiny pieces of paper near the fireplace, while Jane was nibbling on a molasses cookie by the window.

"You must have gotten home late, miss. I went to bed very late, and you were not at home!"

"Aye, Molly."

"Is it Aaron Abbott, the handsome courier?"

"Molly!" A pause. "Perhaps…"

"You be careful, child. Take care of yourself."

"Yes, Molly. He is a gentleman. He has no bawdy intentions, as I can tell. We talk about books and romantic stories, he holds the door for me, and the other day he wrote me a beautiful poem."

"Wrote you a poem? My old boyfriends in Kilkenny did not even know how to write!"

"He called it, 'I am a Caterpillar, You Are a Butterfly.'"

"Oh? You're a butterfly? Move your feet up so I can sweep, butterfly."

"He is so funny and pleasant. Well-mannered. His mother is probably well-mannered."

"Aye. Nobody has ever called me a butterfly before..." Molly sighed. "You enjoy yourself, just do not get overtired."

"Yes, Molly," said Jane.

Jacob and a group of fellow Tory troops were relaxing at a Philadelphia tavern—the Wild Goose—sipping rum and smoking their pipes. It was a rare day off, late afternoon, the sun entering through the three windows that faced to the northwest. Two dogs slept soundly by the giant oak door. The place was nearly empty.

Pratt and Hollins were complaining to the others.

"I don't know about your situations, but me and Pratt are getting pummeled by our Brit superior officers. Pricks!"

Jacob perked up: "What do you mean?"

"They treat us like dogs! They throw their dishes on the floor, they break, and then they charge us for the damage."

"Took it out of our pay," Pratt said.

Hollins said, "My captain threw a fork at me and a Negro, in the mess hall."

"Threw a fork?" Jacob said.

"These men are animals."

"Not all of them, I'm sure. But many. They are frustrated and they are bored." Catlin and Palmer agreed.

"And they are getting sick and tired of war, and this winter camp. Damn kids, rogues. That's all they are."

Jacob: "And they are...taking it out on us, the lowly Tories..."

"Exactly," all agreed and muttered.

"How about you, Jacob, have you experienced any such harassing behavior?" Catlin asked.

Jacob thought a moment and decided to tell a fib.

"Not really. It is fairly quiet and routine down in the jail. I hardly interact with the Brit officers."

"Is that so?"

"Hardly see them at all. I just mop and clean all day, and go home." Jacob wanted to appear strong, and never a victim, to his peers. So he was lying, so what? This was war. Worse things were happening.

"Lucky dog." Pratt sighed.

"We fight for them at Germantown, we march with them! We wear the red."

"And they treat us like colonials. We happened to be born in Jersey or Maryland. What difference does it make?"

"Would be great if we could convince them we were born in England!" someone uttered.

"Impossible. They have records. They know who came over on the ships," Pratt countered.

"Lowly Tories." Jacob sighed. "HEY JENNY! Another round of this *slop*!"

"Yes, boys," the old lady answered.

"Pratt and I were talking yesterday. If this continues, we are walking."

"What? You cannot walk out," Jacob snapped.

"Yes, we can. Others have. We can desert, escape. Hide out."

"And the British turds will never find us. They don't need us anyway. They don't care."

"We would be helping them, less mouths to feed."

"Good heavens. Would you defect over to the Americans?" Jacob asked.

"Christ no! Are you mad? We would desert. We walk."

"Walk, means *walk* Abbott."

"Keep your bloody voices down!" Catlin snapped.

"The Americans? We are crazy, not stupid." Pratt said, chuckling.

"Think about it. Freedom. No more war. Freedom!"

"Freedom," said Catlin.

Jacob drank his rum and thought, his eyes darting side to side. "Aye," he said.

Jenny brought over fresh tankards of rum and water, with sugar and lemon juice.

"Here you go, boys."

"Cheers!" they said. Jacob, Palmer, Pratt, Catlin, and Hollins drank and chatted and looked around, but in a subdued fashion. Were there plans afoot?

Christmas was approaching. The bayberries smelled divine, the holly blew in the breeze, and some of the kids ran around with ice skates tied off in a knot hanging around their neck, some of them go sledding. The theater was doing good business, the pubs, the taverns, the stores. A man had a corner shop that sold replica busts of ancient heroes: Apollo, Caesar, Aristotle, Euripides, Alexander, Medusa, Thomas Aquinas, and Joan of Arc. Next to him was a confectioner who was selling delicious maple candy and other sweets.

All day and night, hundreds of redcoats roamed around, usually a flask in their pocket, darting in and out of the stores, galleries, taverns, and bawdy houses (looking for some temporary company).

Some of the bundled-up children stood outside and rang bells and asked for some charity. Some of them were orphans who lived in the church. And the redcoats usually chided them and laughed at them; it was sad to behold.

"Get a job!" some of them yelled, chuckling.

"Get inside! You'll catch a cold, you runts!"

"Don't matter, they gonna die poor anyways," someone said, chuckling.

"Look how dirty that one is there. You stink! Take a bath!" another one said, chuckling.

"Hey, it's Christmas—show some mercy, will you, sergeant?" Laughter. Sharing their flasks of rum, whiskey. Laughter. Some drunk troops even threw empty bottles at the children, and a few of the scared little ones scattered. More laughter.

A bystander hollered. "Why don't you mind your business, rascals? Dem children didn't do nothin' to you!"

"Shut up, rebel idiot!"

"Bastards…"

Journal entry: *I stroll the gardens for exercise and amusement. Jane is usually with me, but even when not—physically—she really never leaves my thoughts and being. Like a ship that needs deep water. Yesterday we dined at 12 and supped at 8.*

Aaron shaved every day, brushed his teeth, and wore his finest and warmest clothes. He even sprayed fancy French cologne under his arms. His black boots were spotless.

One afternoon they rode horses out of the city to admire the ice forming a canopy over the falls, some 140 feet. A couple artists were also there, capturing it with their brushes. That's when Jane whispered into his ear that she wanted to make love to him, and that he would be her "first time." Aaron said not a word, but smiled, and hugged her in front of the frozen falls.

*****

He felt entirely new things. This was a beautiful woman, one that he adored. He laughed, he kissed, and he rolled around with her, ran his fingers through her hair. She would squeeze him and bite his ears. He rubbed her naked back, he would penetrate her, their fingers would interlock, and she would say to him, "Love me. Love me." Sometimes tiny beads of sweat would rise along her forehead, and a few strands of her luxurious hair would stick to her face. She talked about the Book of Samuel in the Old Testament, she spoke of the Silbermann fortepiano and the Fugue, the fables of Aesop, reading the book *Emily Montague* (1769) by Mrs. Frances Brooke. She was so alive! She used to draw sketches of Rococo bouquets that she read about, and dreamed about, in Paris, and she would show the drawings to her boyfriend from Somerset, usually standing stark naked. She would laugh and smile often, and her green eyes would for a few seconds stand out as the distinguishing feature to her being. She twinkled and then blinked. She was elegant. Aaron saw mystery and pure excitement; he was aroused. He felt. He felt. He liked how she walked and opened doors, and sipped her tea, and how she laughed. He began to feel anxious when they were not together.

He felt. Every new day with her was heaven, and the next one was even better. They dated for two weeks, then three weeks. And then a fourth week. They told each other, *I love you*, and this was a strange sensation for Aaron. He felt. And there was nothing wrong with that.

They would lie naked on the bed together and listen to the booming clang of the church bells, regularly at 7:00 p.m. It spoke out and echoed all through the neighborhood and Vine Street and fell upon Jane's house like it was shot from one of Jacob's cannon.

CHAPTER 4

He would walk outside the paneled doors back to his route, his head spinning and his body glowing with energy. Relax. It's real. Don't think. Embrace it. Embrace it. Don't mess this up. It's real. Have never loved another woman. First time with a woman.

He delivered his mail, but his mind was in Jane's bedroom, with the bright yellow walls, mirrors, pewter dishes, and candles. It had a soft feeling. It had a smell that Aaron had never before smelled. He walked and delivered and walked, in a trance.

The four-post bed was lavish, walnut made, draped with scarlet and white fabric. Her vanity against the wall was incredibly organized, the powders and oils and color. Smelled and looked incredible. Jane was gorgeous and happy. You wanted to crawl into her—that soft smile!—and have a conversation that would last weeks.

She gave him the book *Emily Montague* (1769) by Mrs. Frances Brooke. He loved the book, not only because it was an interesting book but also because it gave off a slight aroma of her fingertips and bedroom, French oils and powders. Simply put, it was Jane's. The words that jumped off the pages seemed different, special.

They made love. They talked about the book. They lost themselves in romance. They laughed. They dated, courted, chatted, discussed, and dreamed. Aaron had found something he never knew existed, and that was—happiness with a lady. A Philadelphia lady, heavens! He walked and delivered and walked, in a trance. Smiling and loose, alive.

He kissed her hips and toes and shoulders, and both of them giggled happily.

"Make love to me," she said.

"Make love to me," she said.

Don't think. Don't think. Be yourself! Happiness with a lady. His body glowed with adrenaline all the time. The machinery in his body was kicking and sprinting—wild horses—and he could function with little sleep. True, deep, thick, his masculinity was spinning a globe; it was like faraway lands. Spinning. In time he would meet her aunt and a few of her friends. At one point, Molly asked the unthinkable to Aaron when Jane was out of earshot: "Are you going to ask for her hand in marriage?"

*****

Officer Tittinger punched Jacob hard in the stomach. Again.
"You like that, Dung?"
Jacob coughed a few times but stood straight. He was surrounded by three redcoats.
"Grab him."
They grabbed Jacob, three guys. It's not like he was going to attempt escape; they had him. The officer then walked over, the floorboards creaked under his boots, and he did the unthinkable.
He pulled out his penis and showed the group. He chuckled.
"What do you think of this, Jersey dung?" he asked.
"Do you like British cock?"
(Laughter.)
Jacob stared straight ahead, motionless, like a stunned animal. This was a sick man, but he wouldn't…he couldn't. He slowly inched forward… He wouldn't.
Officer Tittinger leaned in and spoke right into the American's ear. "This isn't bad treatment, dung. You should see what I do to the Connecticut Tories."
(Laughter.) And mercifully he buttoned up his pants, and he and his crew walked back up the stairs. Jacob, after nearly a minute, rubbed his face with his hands, stood up straight, and walked away appalled. He angrily kicked over his wooden bucket.
"Sir, may I have some water?"
"Shut your bloody mouth!" Jacob yelled toward the cells.

*****

Christmas Eve 1777. Hundreds of redcoats, their families, and/ or mistresses and friends buttoned up their finest attire, slicked their hair, shined their boots, sprayed themselves with their best perfumes, and set off to light up the town. It would be a night filled with laughter, dancing, flirting, and beautiful women! Except for American troops like Jacob. He would not experience the colorful, drunken balls. Jacob was cleaning and mopping the officer's quarters. *Special assignment*, they called it, mockingly. So he arrived around 9:00 p.m. and got to mopping. His only companion in the officer's quarters was sheer boredom, but that was about to change.

"I love you, corporal. Attractive military man you are!"

"I love you, Jane. We are going to be so happy together."

"Even when I get fat?"

"Even then!"

"Imagine if I had never asked you to accompany me to the theater that evening! We would never be together. Oh…"

"That was a merry day indeed. And a great play. You looked beautiful that night, your hair in curls, your shawl, the gown."

"Yes. And look how far we have come, after only four weeks."

"It is like I've known you for four years. This war will be over soon, and when it is, I propose we settle down in Somerset. Huge brick house. A tower of happiness!"

"Our house will be filled with music and laughter and lots of children, darling," she said, her head propped up against goose-feather pillows.

Aaron said, "And whale-oil lamps,"

"Yes!"

"Imported from *Edgars and Price—Fused silverplate Argand-type, with octagonal urn-shaped font, decorated with garlands. The font is affixed to a flared and stepped base that sits atop an integral cylindrical pedestal and spooled foot that screws into a baluster-shaped arm protruding from a circular wall plate affixed with three screws. Attached to the pedestal is a swelled and faceted arm…*"

"Are you reading my magazine again?"

"Yes. Sorry…" Aaron closed a magazine and tossed it down off the bed. They chuckled. She playfully punched his arm. Tickled, he felt now was a good time to broach an irresistible issue.

"One of these fine evenings, I will ask for your hand in marriage."

"And what should I say?" she smiled, her face drawing in close to his.

"You should say yes. At the proper time…"

"Aye, soldier."

"I like it when you call me that."

"You're safe right here with me, soldier. Not out on the battlefield…"

"Right here. With Jane Canterbury."

Aaron had a crazy notion—he could ask her right then, but things were too fast, and he hadn't prepared; it didn't seem romantic. But he wanted to. They started to kiss, and she blew out the candle…

"Merry Christmas, love."

"Merry Christmas, Jane."

*****

Around midnight, the commanding officer, Captain Tittinger, brought back a female companion to the quarters, and drunkenly threw her on the bed. It was a female Indian—perhaps a Lenape Delaware, only in her teens. She was screaming *no* in her native language: "No, no, no!"

He was grunting, and there was an uncomfortable and noisy struggle on the bed. "Shut up!"

Jacob Abbott was two hundred feet away, dumping a bucket of dirty water down the latrine. He immediately heard the commotion and popped his head from the wooden door and peered down the poorly lit hallway, over about thirty beds. The officer slapped her in the face. *Slap.* "Shut up!" He was reaching up her bead-encrusted dress to try to rip it off her. "No, no, no!" she cried.

"Shut up!"

Suddenly, he was taken by two strong arms and forcibly rolled off the bed. A lamp made a loud crash against the wall. The lady stopped shouting for a moment. There was a tall American there, in the shadows. The two men wrestled for a moment, but it was a one-sided affair. Jacob was fueled with anger and aggression and completely sober, while the officer was struggling to stand, with blood-shot eyes. Struggling to land a punch. He squinted his eyes.

"Jersey dung," he said, surprised.

"That's right."

Jacob punched him in the ribs and threw him against the wall, and the man landed in the broken fragments of what had been the lamp. The soldier was beaten. Jacob walked over, grabbed his opponent by the hair, and with a long blade sliced the man's throat and killed him. The lady started to cry. The body dropped to the floor like a sack of flour. Blood flicked onto Jacob's blouse and boots and left hand. The half-naked lady was stunned and silent, having difficulty breathing. Jacob cleaned his blade against his blouse, and quickly hid the body outside in the back of the quarters. The lady looked at Abbott. Abbott looked at her. He methodically pushed fragments of the lamp under the bed. He quickly cleaned off his hands and wiped errant blood off his cheek. Then he darted away, into the night.

Jacob ran across the parade ground, past the latrine, and over to the tent city that was set up, east of the cemetery. Many soldiers were singing and drinking and writing letters to their sweethearts for the holidays. He passed about sixty boys and young men, stepping around little campfires, his head turning quickly left and right and left again, hopping between two hunting dogs, until he finally found who he was looking for.

"A word with you, Palmer, Pratt, Catlin, Hollins."

One of them raised his bottle. "Abbott! Jesus came to earth, my man, and he gave me spiced rum to drink! It's his birthday!"

He took a swig from his brown bottle while Jacob was formulating his words.

"Jesus was born in Bethlehem of Judea in the days of Herod the king, my man! Let's celebrate! I have seen your star!" said one.

"Abbott, I have seen your star, said the Jews!" Laughter.

Jacob motioned with his hands and had a dead-serious look about him. "Gentlemen, I hate to break the party… Gentlemen, quiet! Listen. I am out. Gone. I will explain later."

"What?" they asked, with watery eyes.

"I am out, I am leaving. Now." It was a loud whisper.

"What?"

Jacob grabbed two of them by the jacket. "Wake up, man! I'm in a bit of trouble. I am leaving. Tonight. Right now."

"Are you sure?"

"Quite sure. Things got heated back there. We got in a fight," Jacob said.

"You struck an officer?"

"Shhhh!" he said.

"Yes. They are looking for me. They think I am at the barracks. But I am not. I am flying, boys. Inland!"

They stood up. "We want to come with you."

"Splendid. We must hurry. Grab your sidepieces and some food. Do not mention this to a soul. You have thirty minutes. Try to sober up for Chrissakes… You will meet me at Essex Avenue. Be prepared to go downriver."

"Essex? Are you sure, Abbott?"

"Yes, dammit. And One of you, please summon my brother. Posthaste. We leave tonight!"

> God rest ye, merry Gentlemen,
> Let nothing you dismay,
> For Jesus Christ our Savior
> Was born upon this Day.
> To save poor souls from Satan's power,
> Which long time had gone astray.
> Which brings tidings of comfort and joy.[7]

Several British officers were standing around a campfire, taking some nips off a tiny rum bottle, glow on their faces, hitting all the right notes (in their heads) and simply enjoying their Christmas. This was peace and not war, for a day. No Bunker Hills, no Harlem

Heights, no Fort Lees, and no Billingsport. This was camp life. The guys under the stars, with the trees and the conversations. That edge, although never eliminated, was softened. Many of them were exhausted but not sleepy, not now. They were too busy laughing and ribbing each other and drinking, and celebrating the Feast of the Nativity, or Christmas. Two boys were sitting on tree stumps and both playing the flute, melodies by Jacques-Martin Hotteterre that were decades old. France was of course the enemy, but this French flautist was embraced and loved by nearly all aspiring musicians.

Two officers stepped past the music, out of the shadows, with an eager look on their faces.

"Matthews, where is the captain? He is nowhere to be found."

"I am not sure, sir."

"Go find him. He's gone missing!"

"Yes, sir!"

Matthews sped away toward the officers' quarters, and the two redcoats walked in the opposite direction toward the camp.

"Merry Christmas, gents…"

"Merry Christmas, Sir."

There was a knock on the door.

"Abbott, you in there?"

Aaron and Jane threw the blankets over their bodies and looked at each other.

"Yes. What is it?" Aaron shouted.

"Please meet me in the hallway. There is a problem with your brother Jacob."

He looked at his wife-to-be, a bit unsure. "I don't recognize that voice," he whispered to her.

And she said "Go. Go!" He got dressed, kissed her on the forehead, and darted out with this fellow out the paneled front door and down the cold quiet street. They held a lantern, and it bounced in many directions as they walked rapidly down Vine Street and out of sight. Jane pulled the covers up to her throat and stared at the dark ceiling, feeling afraid. Maybe Jacob was ill, or hurt? Was there a bad accident at the camp?

*****

49

They waited for nightfall. Pratt and Hollins were tasked with procuring a jon boat behind the arsenal, while Palmer had the dangerous mission of igniting an "accidental" fire at the Dutch Calvinist assembly rooms two blocks away—a perfect distance to create the diversion they needed. Jacob and Aaron, it was decided, would steal three horses on the other side of the Schuylkill. Aaron had joined them within the hour.

"What's happening here?" he asked.

"Shhhhhh. Later!" barked Jacob.

Their boat floated southward, toward Wilmington. The boys could smell the pungent stinks of the barrels of tar, salted fish, corn, and split pine boards. It was the cover of night. The tall lighted buildings and chapels of the city lay at their back. Aaron stared in the general direction of Vine Street and thought only of his love Jane, with a heavy melancholy. Anger. After thirty seconds, her neighborhood got that much farther away, slowly and tortuously. They saw some British patrol but no alarm was called; after all, the men wore red jackets, and they were calmly departing the city, and this was not unusual. To enhance the charade even more, Jacob yelled at one of the security: "Call Major Rathbone! A fire has struck on Second Street! I am alerting the colonel." And it worked. The boys on the ledge wheeled around and raced down a dark alley away from the river.

They floated and rowed for one hour, beyond the city limits, and then they silently tied up on the west bank of the river at a place called Gibson Point.

Here Palmer reconnected with the others, and now they were, and felt like, six deserters. Wanted men. It was near eleven at night. The aim was to saddle up, flee through Lancaster County, and hide at the marshes of Conestoga Creek. Once they were beyond the Conestoga, a full seventy miles beyond the reach of the British sentries, they were home free. They had on red coats, and they had an unhurried look about them, and they all six were able and smooth riders. They even said hello to other redcoats on the road. The word had not come down, of course, that a ranking officer had been murdered, and that there was a serious fire in town. In fact, everything seemed a bit lax since it was Christmas. The six of them rode through the night, under the moon and cold calls of the unseen hoot owls. They rode to Chatham, and rode to Chester, and rode to Holtwood Dam at a wide creek bed. They watered the horses, rested for a couple hours, and then continued. On the second night, soft flakes of snow filled the sky and covered the area—farms, wild meadows, thickets, and treetops.

Jacob exchanged his red coat with a dark-green cloak, and instead of his military tricorn he wrapped a scarf around his head; in this, he would not match the description of his fugitive self. They continued to ride, at a medium pace, in utmost silence.

Three days later, Jane Canterbury stood in her upstairs bed-chamber and looked out her window, down onto the stirring Vine. She combed her long hair, and her lips carried a slight frown. Her love had not called on her Tuesday evening, nor sent a note, and now this night appeared to have the same result. Where was he? There was a strange energy to the neighborhood, to the city. Aaron Abbott. Was he injured, was he in trouble, was he on assignment, was he captured? The house was depressingly quiet, save for the distant clicks and taps of Molly putting away the clean dishes downstairs.

Molly soon came into the room with a pile of fresh linen. "We won't have to worry about the Americans. They will soon freeze to death in their camps…"

"I heard they went to camp in Baltimore," Jane said, putting her hair brush away.

"No, dear, they are but twelve miles away, near Chesterbrook. Valley Forge, they call it." A cold gust of wind just then slammed into the glass windows, and the trees outside shook in unison.

"Valley Forge? They *will* freeze to death…"

*****

Jacob Abbott stood tall in his newly acquired buckskin breeches, bare chested, and shaving with a straight edge. He held in his left hand a small piece of glass, using it as a mirror. There was a blast of sunshine on this wintry day; it was a comfortable forty degrees with no wind. The three horses grazed nearby.

"Today's the epiphany." He stroked his face straight down his cheek. In the glass's reflection, he could see his five buddies sitting on the cold dirt against the fence, resting.

Aaron was reading his Bible. He had nightmares the night before that Jane was struggling, that she was worried, and that bad men had taken her away. She was screaming and didn't look beautiful, and of course Aaron had awoken. He was miserable. And she probably was too; he could only imagine.

"Brother, how long until I go back? I have met someone that I'd like to marry."

The others laughed. Aaron found it rather cruel. Jacob said, "In due time. I'm afraid you need to wait, brother. We are wanted men. This war will be over soon..."

"Until?"

Jacob snapped at Aaron. "Until it's safe! It is too dangerous—those raiders and bandits. American spies, British patrols, so you need to wait."

Several times they had to run and hide from British patrols. It had been terrifying and exhausting.

"Can I go back to the city and say goodbye to her?"

"Impossible, brother. I'm sorry." The others chuckled with their eyes closed, drowsing.

Catlin said, "Fellow, don't let a woman pull you around like an ox. She can wait, and you will get back there when it's safe."

"We were planning to wed!" Aaron shouted.

Jacob replied, "I understand. But you must wait! Do you want to get killed?"

Aaron took a step forward. "Tell me what happened back there!"

He finished shaving and put his little mirror away. "I struck an officer," Jacob said.

"Heavens. That's it?" they said.

"Hmm. I may have, actually, ended up...killing the man. My captain."

"Christ."

"Tittinger?" Pratt asked.

"That's right," Jacob confirmed.

"Well, Tittinger is dead. I will sleep well tonight…" one of them uttered.

"Amen," somebody uttered.

"Give me your pipe," he barked at his younger brother. He took a few puffs and looked behind them along the horizon to make sure they were safe, for now.

"You are certain?" Pratt asked.

"Trust me," Jacob said. Aaron sat back down on the cold ground with the others. A couple of them were blowing warm air into their chilled hands. Jacob, the acknowledged leader, put on his shirt and put the blade away. He was about four years older than the others here.

"Gentlemen, today's the epiphany. The wise men have paid us a visit. They told us, like the magi, to follow the star. I want to thank you for your courage and dependability over the last two weeks. You made the right decision in fleeing that hell-pit camp. We have survived, and we are free, thanks to you and your intelligence and teamwork. You are good soldiers. You are fine men. But suffice it to say we are wanted men. We are not out of danger. Just yesterday I killed another bandit from those woods, maybe a spy. They are looking for us. Must be some price for our heads. We need to check our ammunition and supplies, because we need to pull out of this location."

"Aye," they said.

"Gentlemen, I propose we split up. It's too dangerous to remain packed as one. We need to show speed and flexibility. We are free. I propose—my dear brother and I stay together and move over the creek toward the Susquehanna and turn north."

"But—"

"And when this damn war is over, we head back to Philadelphia. Mother can return home again! And Aaron can marry his sweetheart."

The boys chuckled…

"Sure, Jacob. We must stay out here hidden. But for many months?" Pratt asked.

"It may be a few months, it may be a year. But I see it happening. The damn rebels need to be destroyed. Washington as a general is a damn joke. We showed our loyalty to the king, and the British will triumph, like in nearly every conflict that came before. I can sense it."

"Even when the British win the war, you will still stand trial for that felony committed, eh?" said Hollins.

"Perhaps. I will face that predicament when the time comes. In any case, you should decide what you will do and where you will go. It is imperative that whatever happens, to any of us, that not a word is spoken about our flight from Philadelphia. Not a word."

"Aye, not a word," they muttered.

"And with any luck, I will see each and every one of you in Philadelphia, after the grand victory, by the end of the year."

The boys smiled.

"Yes," said Jacob.

"We're wanted men. No one's going back to Philadelphia for at least a year."

Aaron slammed down his pipe, held his head in his hand, disgusted and sad. *She has no idea of my whereabouts… A year!*

Jacob and Aaron got together and counted their money; they had sixteen pounds, nine shillings, and Spanish silver pieces, etc. Sizeable. They give Catlin and Hollins and Pratt and Palmer some money and supplies. They wished each other good luck. They had dinner by a small fire. Hollins said, "Brothers, bring your hands in a circle, take this knife, and mark our commitment with blood!" Jacob liked the idea, but Aaron needed convincing. They sliced their six palms, some blood was produced, and they clasped their fingers and hands. Good-luck brothers. The blood melded together in a dark red concoction; some of it was dripping off Aaron's wrist.

"Love you, brothers!"

"Love you, brothers…"

After dinner, they all ran away. Fresh flakes blanketed the region. The muddy puddles along the old cart paths turned solid ice.

CHAPTER 5

"Molly, I think I am going crazy," said Jane.

"Why, butterfly?"

"Something terrible is happening. I am afraid. Some men came to the house and pulled Aaron away and said there was a problem with his brother. And he held my hand, but I told him to go, so he kissed me and—"

"A problem with his brother? There's nothing in the news. We shall go down to the camp and inquire about it."

"I may never see him again. Molly, I have been having nightmares! What if they killed him?"

"Calm down, calm down. Nobody killed him. He's probably on some crazy, last-minute assignment. Or maybe a part of the Army had to—relocate."

"You think so?"

"I think so. You know the British brass—tons of money and recklessly impulsive…"

"We were planning to wed. Husband and wife…" she said quietly.

"The news comes tomorrow. We will check to see if his outfit set off on detail. Do not despair."

"All right, Molly."

"Very good. Now clean up and get dressed. We need to go downtown and get your boots cleaned, and I need some new plated buckles from Booth's."

*****

The local news bulletins meanwhile described in detail those "wretched deserters from the king's Army, Fourth Pennsylvania artillery unit"—Pratt, Abbott, Hollins, Catlin, Palmer—with full descriptions and best guesses to where they might be found, and a handsome reward for any information.

Catlin and Hollins set out before dawn the next morning, heading south and west, their aim to land at the mouth of the Chesapeake Bay, perhaps a week's march away. Hollins had relatives in Annapolis, the old capital city. They spent a few nights next to a lake, and then kept marching south. The temperature stayed comfortable. They would quickly bathe themselves in the streams, and nibble on what was available to them—berries, jerky. On the fifth night, there was a scary moment when their peaceful and warm campfire was surrounded, at the black of night, by hungry wolves. The beasts smelled the dead rabbits that were hanging on the spit. Catlin fired his rifle into the sky, and the wolves scattered. Two weeks out, Catlin and Hollins spent a night at a tavern at Havre de Grace. They got a needed rest, a shave, and a good meal. Hollins paid a prostitute for her services. The place was teeming with businessmen and travelers, and Blacks and pirates and priests, and soldiers on both sides. It wasn't safe. Catlin and Hollins, both about eighteen, were wanted men. They risked fate. They inquired about water transport to Annapolis. The next barge would leave on February 1, they were told. "Tickets are to be had at nine of the clock, departure set for eleven." They kept a low profile and slunk away in a back corner of the tavern. They sipped drinks and eyed an elderly fellow—was he eighty?—who sat, with a gray feline in his lap. The old man had one hand missing, white hair, green trench.

"You two should smile. You have both your bloody hands. Look at me!"

"Aye, sir. Normally I would be smiling, but we are so tired."

"Tired. Tired of what? Your old ladies bossing ye around?"

"Tired of the war, man."

"War? What do you know about war? You been in battle?"

"Yes, sir. Germantown."

"HA! That's not battle. That's just a bunch of pretty lads prancing around with little shiny toys."

"All due resp—"

The old man said, "I have been to war, brothers! Got my damn hand ripped off! In 1759. I was in the Navy."

"Oh?"

"Aye. The French took it right off, at the invasion of Martinique." There was a pause.

"Ye ain't never heard of it, have ye?"

"Afraid not, sir."

"That's because it ain't in your history books yet! I faced off against ten thousand French marines, and I wasn't afraid. It was hot and humid, and me and my men hadn't had a meal in two weeks! There were crabs everywhere the size of that lady's ass right there."

Catlin and Hollins looked at each other and grinned.

"I jumped ship and charged the iron gates. Must have killed me about twenty or thirty of dem bastards. Au revoir, maggots. Got my face cut up, took a number of bullets. And they sliced off my hand with a French saber. It was my favorite hand!"

"Oh…" the boys uttered.

"Aye. Say, buy me a drink? Two good soldiers to one old one…"

"Yes, sure."

Hollins got up and walked to one of the staff, who was pouring drinks into a large wooden pitcher. "What is it, son?"

"Three of those ales if you please, for me, my friend, and the wounded warrior in the corner."

"Wounded warrior, huh?" the barman repeated.

"Yes."

"Let me guess. He is talking about the invasion of Martinique?"

"Aye. That's right."

"And the French cut off his hand?"

"Aye. Quite a battle."

"Son—that's Frederick, he lives here. A retired cooper. He's never left Maryland in his life!"

The patrons at the bar all loudly laughed and chuckled. One of them raised their glass and yelled, "Martinique! Get 'em, Frederick!" (Laughter.)

The old man smiled, took his ale from Hollins, and took a sip, and then yelled back, "It got me a free beer!"

*****

Pratt and Palmer, meanwhile, trekked west and north, sleeping in several barns and pens along the way. On the fifth night they caught some perch and dined handsomely on this. They also met some Indians and traded their smooth "civilized" pipes for their freshly bagged deer. They marched and slept, slept and marched. After two weeks, they climbed up Hawk Mountain and camped. But the weather snapped cold and unbearable at this altitude, and the boys built huge fires and widened their search for wild game. They were starving. The sky was thick with freezing rain and sleet, coming in at odd angles. They made natural tents out of tree branches and shrubbery and did their best to stay dry. The wild grass got so cold and hard; it made a snapping sound when you trekked across. All the bunnies and wolves were hidden and cozy. Palmer's stomach had upset him; he complained that the deer they purchased from the Indians was rotten or tainted. He vomited for a few days. They had no medicine. Dehydrated, they waited and suffered up on the mountain. They were both about sixteen. They were scared, felt they had run out of options. They felt like they were surrounded. There was probably a handsome reward for their capture. Late at night, they would detect sudden scurrying movements through dead leaves and over broken sticks, down below. Deer? Boar? Random hikers or travelers? They knew better. One night, Pratt was captured by an American patrol and marched down the mountain, and Palmer— alone, cold, and hungry—committed suicide. The gunshot was sudden and loud from the dark summit, the turkey buzzards scattering into the sky. Later, some men found Palmer's journal, and on the back page it was written in an unsteady hand: *Soon it will be February 1, 1778. In the name of our Lord and king. But I will be dead. I was born in 1761 in New York. Forgive me father, for the ball will hit its intended mark…*

The war records, ironically, showed both Pratt and Palmer as brave heroes who fought valiantly at Germantown for His Majesty's Army, whipping the enemy, and helping to preserve England's iron hold of its colonial possessions and thwarting any chance of rebellion. Two men who shone in battle. Palmer was dead, and Pratt would die on a prison ship of dysentery the very next year. The group who had captured poor Pratt received a reward of sixty American dollars.

Seven American colonials emerged from the woods in Somerset, New Jersey, each carrying bundles of long sticks and chunks of wood. They walked and chatted as if they were strolling along a boardwalk on a pleasant summer's day. They walked to one side of the house and came up upon a shattered window; one of their group was standing inside that could be seen through the opening. Taking turns, they fed him their respective scraps of wood. The man on the inside created a large, circular fire lay and it came up to his waist. It was dry and vibrant. He sprinkled some linseed oil, a bit here, a bit there, making a smaller moist circle within the larger circle of dry timber. He produced a little flame and dropped it carefully into his creation and took a step backward and watched science take over—the small yellow breaths, the orange gasps, and after three minutes a blaze that shouted out yellows and oranges with whites and blues, and the man for good measure tossed the 1763 side table once belonging to Ms. Lindsay Abbott right on top of the monster—the cherry legs caught quickly—and then he hopped out the window. It grew quite hot, of course. He knew his concoction would soon reach out and infect the old pine floors, which would climb up the walls, and within forty minutes the roof would be strangled. And within forty minutes more, the Abbott home in Somerset where Jacob, Aaron, Charlotte, and Eliza grew up with their mom would collapse in charred agony. *Death to Tories.* Dante's poem. Destroyed. It was the house the girls sang in and fell down the stairs, the house where Jacob carved his first chicken at table, the house where Aaron did a clumsy somersault in the hall and knocked over a fancy piece of pottery and heard it smash, and then the same house where his dad whipped him with the belt and told him to stop horsing around. The flames spread and jumped and climbed, and soon pulled everything down to the hot earth. By that time, the pyromaniacal Americans were long distant, hunting their next prey.

*****

The clerk at the Havre de Grace ferry soon reported to his superiors the unusual, smelly boys who claimed to be "travelling mechanics." Those superiors reported to a local adjutant, and on February 1, Catlin and Hollins were cornered and captured by Maryland militia. They were taken prisoners to Smithfield. It was a hellish experience. Every day they drank dirty water and lumpy gray gruel, with bugs inside it. They cursed their decisions in life, the war, and the British and Americans. Why did we fight? Why did we escape? Why are we at Smithfield? They both were hoping that the British would strike a death blow and the Americans would surrender, and these prison camps would be liberated. But it didn't want to happen. Washington and Lafayette didn't allow that to happen. And so it went. Within six months, they would both be dead by the treacherous smallpox. Their families and girlfriends never actually found out. In the ensuing decades, Catlin and Hollins were listed only as MIA from their units in Philadelphia. Heroes at Germantown.

The woods were teeming with British and Americans and Indians, bounty hunters, bandits, spies, criminals, and opportunists—all looking for people just like Jacob Abbott, murderer. The boys were in a tight spot. It was worse than originally thought. Spending so much time along the Atlantic seaboard clouded their thinking that those hills out on the horizon were a peaceful refuge to wait out the war.

Aaron was in deep melancholy for Jane. Jacob did a fair trade with some passing Indians—he gave them his rifle (keeping his pistol) in return for ginseng, bags of corn, tobacco, and three woven blankets. As if to apologize for their current plight, Jacob handed his little brother the sack of sweet Orinoco, fresh from the earth. They grinned at one another.

Aaron opened the top and took a sniff. "This would fetch ten shillings back in Somerset."

"For certain."

About one-fourth mile in the distance, some dogs were barking. Aaron leaned forward and his packed his pipe.

"Brother." Jacob began.

"Yes?"

"I'm sorry I pulled you into this. We are not safe here. Brother, we have to get to Canada."

Flakes of snow blew quickly across the sky. The clouds floated over the ridge, and rime ice formed when water droplets in clouds froze to the trees. It gave the region an extra sparkle.

Aaron pulled his scarf around his head and leaned against the corner of a barn that seemed out of the wind.

The next two days were not pleasant. The boys tried to sleep on the frosty ground with the blankets from the Indians. They scurried about six miles a day. Their backs and muscles ached. They hid behind large sheds and barns aplenty—most barns in Pennsylvania had the trademark gambrel roof. They passed Dutch, Germans, and Swiss, also Indians and free Blacks. It snowed. The boys shot some rabbits and cooked them. Jacob pulsed with intensity and didn't slow a step. He shaved every day and thought about where he wanted to be tomorrow, but always looking behind him in case they were being followed. His gun was always loaded and ready.

"Brother..."

"Yes?" Aaron said.

"Let this be another lesson for ye..." As Jacob spoke, an icy puff of air was released from his strong face.

"What's that?"

"Never. Never—never walk around with an unloaded weapon. A situation might suddenly present itself."

"Got it, brother," Aaron said.

"You know I had this bad dream last night. And I never have bad dreams. It was unwelcome..."

"What was it?" Aaron asked.

"Well, I don't remember the details. I just have concerns about Mother and my sisters. What if they never made it to England? What if something happened to them? Spanish, Dutch, Americans dotting the ocean. I would say, they had an 80 percent chance of making it. Maybe 75…"

"Let us say 80. I hear ye. I have the same concerns. But I think they made it. The Lord is with our family."

"Aye. You seem assured, brother," said Jacob.

"My bad dreams are different. It's about Somerset and our lives, and friends. Will the town and county and our land, and our beautiful house, be forever changed? This war is a black mark, Jacob. I have this dream. I am asleep at our home like a normal night, but a hideous tsunami comes from the Jersey Shore and envelopes us. We are surrounded by water, underneath us water, and our house fades out into the ocean. We are all asleep, the house is intact, but all I see for miles and miles, everywhere, is ocean."

"Sounds pretty lonesome."

"Rudderless."

"It is safe to say, we may have to settle somewhere else, after the war. You will have a woman anyways."

"We'll see. This adventure is not helping our relationship."

They laugh. "It is keeping you alive."

"Aye."

"This damn war has thrown everything off-kilter."

"Changing subject," said Aaron.

"What is it?" asked Jacob.

"Do you remember, when you were a boy, one of any great conversations with Father, before he passed, that has stuck with you?"

"Aye. *Talk some sense into your little brother!*"

"Ha. Seriously," said Aaron. He poked the hot fire with the heel of his boot and stared at the orange embers expose themselves.

"Treat everyone with respect. Do what is right." A pause. "Serve your community. And fear nothing, except the fear of God. The fear of the *Lord* is the beginning of wisdom," he said. A pause. "Plus, he taught me how to skin a possum and rabbit."

"I wish I remember those talks. I was too young."

"Aye. I think I was twelve when he passed. Sisters were but babes in the crib. Mother cried for a long time. Shut her door, and I could hear her crying loudly from the hall. Father was a great man."

"Aye."

"He told me he understood my personality and my young drive—I could hunt and fish, and I could defend myself like a good young'n. But one day, he told me, he didn't—"

"What?" demanded Aaron.

A pause. "He didn't know if you had that same inner strength of purpose to overcome adversity and reach success in this world. He was quoting the Bible about steadfast mind, or something."

Aaron said, "Isaiah 26: Those of steadfast mind you keep in peace—because they trust in you. Trust in..." A pause. "The Lord forever, for in the Lord God..." A pause. "You have an everlasting rock. He told you that?"

"Aye."

"Why didn't you ever tell me?"

"The situation never warranted it," Jacob answered.

"Well, the only thing to do is to show him. I will show him. I am an Abbott just as you are."

"Cool down. Just keep your powder dry and move rapidly and listen to me. You will be fine."

Aaron said, "I will be fine, more than fine! I could have fought at Germantown like you. They just put me at courier, but I was ready. I went through training with all the other boys!"

"Calm down. You will get your chance one day. And then you will show them. Keep your bloody voice down. Bury that carcass and go fetch us some water, and then clean the knives. We leave in ninety minutes."

"Aye," sighed Aaron.

In contrast with Jacob, Aaron was starting to feel sluggish, in addition to being miserable; he was sick for his Jane and perhaps was in the midst of a breakdown of sorts. He had a heavy cold in his chest and nose. Although neither of the boys wanted to admit it, he was holding up the escape. It seemed that the more Jacob talked and planned—and each puddle he leaped over—his little brother got more and more quiet, showed less interest in the days ahead, and would rest more and more, as Jacob wanted to trot. Aaron had had Jane in his fingers, only weeks ago, his life was set. Dimples, hair, laughter... Now he was out here, in the frozen slush, running from the British, just trying to survive. Maybe the war would end.

Maybe the war would end. Philadelphia was only 98 miles to the east. Jane Canterbury. Jane Canterbury. Now, 103 miles, and 109 miles—they were going in the wrong bloody direction.

Journal: *March 1 78. Maybe the war would end...*

They had passed over and around handsome properties owned by Weigel, then Hager, then Leiker. And then Meiser, and also Heidler. Run, trot, walk, rest. Hide from armed soldiers on horseback. Trot, rest, run. Hide behind another large wooden barn. Getting cold. Sleep (very badly). It was not uncommon in this region for people to have deer as pets. The brothers saw the domesticated creatures walking in and out of peoples' little huts as if an old family member. One had to be careful out here and always think twice before you pulled the trigger.

At 6:00 a.m. the next morning, Jacob woke up Aaron and said, "Get your gear. Let's go!"

CHAPTER 6

The boys were recuperating in an old shed about one hundred paces behind a water mill, which smelled like varnish and sulfur. The air felt thick like a heavy rain was coming. Aaron had sat himself down in a corner, exhausted. His hands, however, stayed busy as he was carving a deer antler into a spoon, or what would become a spoon. He at this moment was thinking about his mother and sisters and grew melancholy at their fate. Surely, they were in England, but where? What would they think if they knew what was happening to us boys? Was this war…or lunacy? Communication was impossible. Life as a fugitive. The deer-antler spoon looked more tired than he was used to. Everything did.

Jacob was standing and looking out one of the small openings, and a sliver of daylight made a marked line down his round hat with feather and on his leggings.

He slowly pulled out his big blade from its leather sheath, looked over at Aaron, and pressed himself against the wall. He made a silent but unmistakable gesture to *don't make a sound.* After a couple excruciating seconds, Aaron heard slow footsteps coming to the shed, growing louder and more pronounced. He looked at Jacob with great trepidation. Jacob resembled a stone statue, one arm cocked. He swallowed.

Jacob sprang across like a great cat and quickly overwhelmed this fellow, pulling him into the shed with his greasy hand firmly over the man's mouth. The man was a free Black who worked at this farmstead, who had departed the water mill to look for some spare buckets.

Aaron of course got to his feet but offered little help. His brother was doing just fine, as he pointed the blade at this utterly confused man as a dire warning. The boy initially kicked his legs a few times, but now stopped and looked at his captor and over at Aaron.

"I want to keep this quiet…will you keep this quiet?" Jacob whispered, intensely. His eyes burned with ferocity.

The Black looked at both boys and said nothing, staring at the steel blade between his eyes.

"You hear me, miller boy?"

"Yes… Who are you?" the boy uttered quietly.

"We're British officers from the Jerseys, just passing through."

"The Jerseys?"

Not having time for chitchat, Jacob got to the point. "Listen—we're heading to Swatara Creek. Do you know it?"

"Do you know Swatara Creek?" he repeated.

"Yes. It's about eleven miles up, right past Jonestown," the boy said.

"What direction?"

He thought a moment. "Go past the mill, through dem trees"—he motioned with his hand—"walk up the creek bed a mile, and y'all see a main road to Jonestown. That road goes right up to Swatara. You'll see it."

"You're certain?" Jacob asked.

"Certain."

"I'm going to put my knife away. You promise you won't run off?" The man didn't answer, and Jacob interpreted this as an affirmative response. Both parties stayed calm. Jacob and Aaron exchanged looks.

Jacob returned his huge knife back to its compartment and gazed a moment out through the shed. "Me and my brother have been through a bit of heavy fortune. Sorry for surprising you like I did. Fighting this damn war makes me mean."

The boy said nothing but exuded calmness.

"Being extra careful." Jacob grinned. The boy grinned for a split second.

Jacob thanked the boy. Aaron also expressed his gratitude, and they made some small talk.

"Who do you work for, boy?"

"Mr. Runyan."

"You a good worker?

"Yes, sir."

"You're a good man. Good man."

Jacob, all the while, kept one eye on the path to the mill, in case there were any signs of a search party. They gave the man some good venison and a vial of some fine rum and made him promise that he would never say a word about this incident. For good measure, Aaron gave him a Spanish coin.

"No problem, officers."

"Thank you, boy."

The Black miller casually returned to the mill. Aaron fell asleep in the shed, but Jacob stood his post and watched the vicinity like a hawk. At one point, he saw the black miller talk to one of the bosses, but all was well. The boss investigated the miller's buckets, said a few sentences, and walked away. Neither of them looked over in the Abbotts' direction.

At dusk, Jacob and Aaron scurried past the mill, through the trees, and found the creek bed, which was described to them. The evening was silent; the moon was gorgeous. There were no signs that anyone knew anything about these fugitives. All was quiet. They slept near Jonestown.

The next several days, they passed through and around large wheat fields and stone mills and streams, as winter was concluding. At one particular stop, Aaron saw men working with cant hooks to fasten felled hemlock and poplar and spruce. The logs were enormous. One would never realize there was a major war on; to these field hands, nothing else mattered except getting their work done before sundown. They made about six or eight miles a day. They passed Evan Pond and saw fat hogs in a field with no fences or barriers to speak of. Every so often, cock pheasants would dart quickly out of the prickly hedges.

Aaron dumped some raw kindling down and watched the yellow-orange flames grow to three feet. The fire popped and hissed. It was quite comfortable out here. Jacob was tearing off a piece of jerky and sipping from his canteen.

Jacob sat down and said, "Say, I hope Pratt and Hollins and those boys made it okay. Still have that scar on my hand."

"Same." Aaron held up his hand. There was a brief melancholy moment, in which the boys had to face facts and presume those four fellow deserters probably did not make it.

Jacob said, "Tell me, what do you think happened to them, brother?" He had a wry grin, and Aaron decided to have a little fun.

"Hollins is probably living on a luxury ship on the Chesapeake, eating fresh oysters and mussels, and has three or four concubines. Enjoying back massages. Pratt—lives in a thirty-room mansion in Baltimore made of stone, has twenty-five Arabian mares, hundreds of pounds in the bank. Catlin is in *Paris*—world-famous artist, hundreds of pounds in the bank. World famous, like…"

"Rembrandt?"

"Exactly. Like Rembrandt. And who am I forgetting—Hollins?"

"No, you said Hollins. It's Palmer," Jacob said.

"Oh yes. Palmer!" Aaron hollered playfully.

Suddenly, the scene was interrupted by an old lady stepping in and holding steady her long loaded rifle at the boys; she was in her late seventies, perhaps eighty. She was thin like a child, wearing a straw hat, fingerless gloves on her hands. The boys politely raised their hands and waited.

"This here's my property. You're trespassing!" she said.

"Uh. Well—" they muttered.

"Who are you?" she said.

"Much respect, ma'am. We are brothers, the Abbotts."

"Abbotts? I don't know no Abbotts!"

"We're from New Jersey."

"New Jersey! That is good reason to shoot you idiots."

Jacob spoke nonthreateningly: "My brother and I are heading up to Canada and wanted to rest, here in this meadow. Be it your meadow, madam?"

"It *is* my damn meadow! This is the Tyson farm. I am Penny Tyson. Git outta here!"

Aaron spoke up. "We apologize, Ms. Tyson. We thought this was a wild meadow between two farms. You must understand. Perhaps, seeing that we have trespassed and disrespected your personal rights, you will accept an *Abbott* apology, to the tune of…three livres. And we'll be out in the morning."

After a quick thought, Penny said, "Three my left foot. Six!" she pointed the gun at Aaron's face.

Jacob said, "How about *five* livres, and you can have a snack with us, and a smoke of New Jersey tobacco?"

"The fire is warm," Aaron said, pointing out the obvious. "We have a seat for ye!"

"Give me the damn money," she said.

Aaron paid her. She set the weapon down and sat herself down. "Give me some of that jerky, boy."

Jacob obliged. The three of them spent an awkward minute staring at the fire and chewing their snack.

"Did you say *Canada*? Ya'll freeze your peckers off!"

"Ha, maybe we shall arrive in the warmer months," Jacob offered.

"You have a lovely meadow, Ms. Tyson…" Aaron said.

"Shut up, young'n. We've had it for three generations now. My husband done died. My sons will take it over and run it. But they are off fighting the war. Don't know if they are safe."

"Oh?" Aaron asked.

"Did you see any of the war?"

"Yes and no, it's complicated," Jacob fibbed.

"What does that mean?" she asked.

Aaron quickly pivoted and asked about *her* boys.

"The last we heard was, they sent a bunch of boys up the Hudson River, above New York, and they are getting together with some Poland fellows up there on order from General Washington. They went up there."

"What for?"

"My neighbor done said, they are building an iron *chain* to block the river. Gonna weigh seventy-five tons!"

"An iron chain to block the river?" Jacob asked.

"Quite a project. Seems like it would sink to the bottom?" Aaron thought aloud.

"Well, the Poland fellows will figure that out. That is why they brought them Poland fellows in. They are engineers!"

Aaron and Jacob looked at each other, and Aaron guessed—"Pulaski? Kosciusko?"

"Interesting. The British will be blocked from coming down," Jacob said.

"No, from coming up. They are in New York already, brother."

"Yes. They cannot come up or down! That's what I said."

"That's not what you said."

"Shut up, Aaron," Jacob snapped.

"Fellas! Be quiet. Give me a smoke of that Jersey stuff," the old lady snapped.

"My sons have been in the fight since seventy-six. Made me proud, they did." She lit it and puffed and smiled.

"Indeed. Has a nice kick—"

"True heroes," Jacob said, with a Tory sense of irony.

"But it's taken a toll on us here in the valley. Manpower is way down. Prices have gone up. The economy is staggering, I tell ye. Impossible to keep up and pay our debts. All the boys and men are gone! I cannot fell dem trees and harvest dem crops. Maybe thirty years ago I could. Not no more. I am in my seventies!"

"Inflation," said Aaron.

"What is that?"

"What you said. They call that inflation. Prices go up, but our money—the currency—is losing its value."

"Are you one of dem Harvard men?" she asked.

"No, I just—"

"Are you alone here, currently?" Jacob asked, changing the subject.

"No. My sisters, their children, two cousins. A couple neighbors also living with us. Everybody is doing their part. One of the kids is sick, and we cannot afford the doctor. Sad. I think we may lose her. And we try to make ends meet. We try…"

"A lot of that going around." Jacob sighed.

"You understand all that *inflation, boy?*" she joked. She chuckled. She handed the pipe back to Aaron, and the lad dutifully wiped it off using his soiled shirt.

"Aye. Try to make ends meet, madam Tyson," Aaron said.

"Aye."

"Well, thank you for the smoke, boys." She stood up and grabbed her gun. "Ya'll can stay for a while but best git outta here in the morn'n."

"Yes, Ms. Tyson."

"And I want that fire you got—completely burned out."

"Yes, ma'am."

"Should have charged you six livres, burning a hole in my meadow!"

"We will clean it up. You'll never know we was here!" Jacob offered.

"Best of luck to you, boys," she said.

"You too, Madam Tyson."

The boys stood up and did a half bow and tipped their caps, as Penny walked away, back up the hill, toward the tiny farmstead. After a minute, Aaron remembered something.

"And Palmer! Palmer has made general, and he has whipped Greene and Sullivan and Washington, and he is about to win the war for our side. Three or four concubines. Big house."

"And hundreds of pounds in the bank," Jacob said. He chuckled, and at the same time Aaron started coughing loudly and spit into the fire. They both laughed.

Meanwhile Jane wrote a letter to her uncle in Delaware. She then picked up a newspaper and read about the villain John Graves Tayloe who led an attack on Judge William Hancock's house during a foraging expedition opposed by Patriot militia. The attack killed ten militiamen in their sleep and wounded several others. William Hancock was also killed, although he was not with the Americans. The attack took place at night and with bayonets. She started to cry. She looked out the window and thought of her lost love. *He was going to marry me.* They were lovers. Everything was set. *And now, everything is in utter ruin. This war has destroyed everything I care for; I have nothing else to live for. I opened myself up to him that night: emotionally, physically, spiritually. And what do we have? The night disappears, a tiny spark of the flint doused with buckets of cold water, no more spark. After several days go by one wonders—was there ever a spark? A night? Was it a dream?* She would lie on her bed, the door locked, thinking about Aaron Abbott. The knight. They met December 3. He disappeared January 4. They saw each other almost thirty-one days in a row!

Meanwhile, the ragtag Continental Army under Washington struggled and shivered north of the city at Valley Forge. The air was filled with scents of bayberry, cooking grease in iron skillets, cow manure, and the smelting from the blast furnaces—cooked metal, cooked iron, heated cobblestone, and thick black smoke that wrestled deftly inside the frigid cold winds that whipped across eastern Pennsylvania.

Lafayette, several Frenchmen, Von Steuben, other Europeans—with the Americans—marched and drilled and marched and drilled and got tougher; they were forged into a disciplined force. Washington rode up and down the lines with a stoic and almost-wooden demeanor. It was early spring 1778. Just down the lane from the main camp, the Seneca and Delaware people hunted and fished, living in modest huts, raising families. Overall, they had enough to eat, but the real problems were lack of supplies and a lack of hard currency that was worth anything.

Almost all the loyalist families had left the mid-Atlantic region by 1778; it was simply too dangerous for them to stay behind. Many, with limited means, went to Canada. Those wealthy enough crossed the ocean blue and landed in Europe, to wait. And hope and pray.

For about twenty-five years, there were always Abbotts living peaceably in Somerset County, about the halfway point between Philadelphia and New York. Jacob and Aaron's father built the place in about 1756, the boys lived there for years with their mother and sisters, of course. But all that changed when the British took Philadelphia.

Ruin. Tears. Anxiety. She was heartbroken; the house on Vine Street was lonely. Information was wanting, but nobody had any. She tried to read her books but could not concentrate on the sentences.

The days seemed to last forever. But one day she finally received some company.

John Graves Tayloe stood in the parlor on the fancy house on Vine Street. He knocked a bit of snow off his hat, he wiped his boots, and then gave a firm knock on the bedroom door. Jane opened it.

"Madam. Do you mind if I ask you some questions on behalf of the king's Army?"

"I don't mind," she said nervously. This was the man from the article, the Hancock raid!

"Jane Canterbury?"

"Yes, sir."

"How long have you lived here?"

"Almost two years."

"And you live with your grandparents and maid?"

"Yes."

"The Phillipses." Tayloe was reading from his official sheet.

"Yes."

"And the maid's name?"

Jane said, "Molly Kildare."

"You are currently unmarried, correct?"

"That is correct."

"Do you have any friends or acquaintances who currently fight for the American side of this struggle?"

"No."

"Are you certain Ms. Canterbury?"

"For certain!"

"Have you made any friends with British soldiers then?"

(There was no answer.)

"Besides me." He laughed…

Jane, remaining quiet, wiped fresh tears from her eyes. Then she let herself cry for a bit. Tayloe didn't blink.

"Miss, I will make it easier for you. Have you befriended one Jacob Abbott, of the Fourth Penn artillery? Raised in Somerset in the Jerseys?"

He looked nervous…"Well…"

"It's all right. Take your time."

"Well, I befriended his brother. Aaron Abbott."

"Hmmmm, brother." There was tension. Silence. It was tense. He glanced down at his notes and then folded them and put in his pocket.

The imposing officer stepped out, talked to other officers who were in the hallway; those men marched down the stairs. John Graves Tayloe calmly came back and this time shut the door. His face was completely blank, stone-cold.

Jane spoke up. "Is there a problem? Aaron fights for His Majesty's Army. He is an able courier."

Tayloe raised his hand and punched Jane across the face, and she fell to the floor in surprise and pain.

"He's gone! He left you, bitch!" he yelled.

He hit her again. Jane was in shock, gasping for air. He hit her a third time. All of these landed right under the eye. Jane was on the floor, feeling defeated. Gasping for her breath. She raised her arm in defense.

She struggled to say, "They said... He is on assignment...and he'll be back!" She sobbed.

"I beg to differ, madam. Nobody said that."

"He's a good soldier!" she screamed.

Tayloe threw down a candle, and it smashed and crumbled across the floor. He violently cracked a mirror at eye level with his elbow.

"Jacob and Aaron Abbott defected!" he yelled in her face.

"Nooooooooooooo, not possible. He's here...somewhere! He's here."

He said, "They are wanted men. The search parties are out. And when we capture those boys, may God have mercy on their soul. Tory scum..."

Jane was crying. Tayloe stood over her like a true villain.

"Stop crying. Listen to me. Stop. Are you listening to me?"

"Yes," she said quietly.

"Your relationship with Jacob and Aaron is forever finished."

She cried louder.

"They will be soon dead. No one leaves *my army!*" he screamed. She cried. "Now As for you—"

"You are banished to North Carolina, forever. You aided and abetted a turncoat. *Aaron Abbott.* You have forty-eight hours to get your most essential items, make travel arrangements, and leave this city."

"No!" she sobbed.

He grabbed her by the hair and pulled out a knife. She cried.

"And you will relocate to North Carolina. Unless—that is—you want to be mutilated and destroyed and ruined, with those nice breasts of yours cut up with this knife. Do you understand?" He pressed the blade against her cheek.

"Do you understand?"

"Yes."

"Where are you going?"

"North Carolina."

"When are you leaving?"

"Within forty-eight hours, sir."

"Very good. Compared to the Abbott boys, you will make off fairly well." He half-smiled.

He dug into his pocket. Jane sat herself up against the wall and stared at the floor. She was tenderly touching the fresh bulge under her eye.

He spoke: "The British Army…would like to assist you in your enterprise." He handed her a pouch of some silver and about eight pounds sterling.

"Good luck on your journey, and I wish to apologize for the bruises on your face. Good day."

"Yes," she said quietly.

"God save the king."

"God save the king," she echoed.

Tayloe left and slammed the door. Jane remained on the floor—red-faced, embarrassed, hurt, and in shock. In an instant Molly darted into the room, found Jane, dropped to her knees, and the two of them hugged tightly, with Jane Canterbury crying and unleashing raw emotion into Molly's shoulder…

"I love him. I love him and he's gone. He was going to marry me. Never…"

She slowly got up and then stared out the window down on the street and watched Tayloe and his men leave the area and walk out of frame. And then they together began picking up pieces of the broken candle. Molly wet a cloth with cold water, and they applied it to Jane's face.

"Molly, we need to go…"

Molly asked, "When?"

*****

They came to a wide sparkling stream and saw two old local fishermen, who thankfully spoke fine English. The sunlight exploded off the top of the slow-moving water. Tiny bugs danced along the edge. Other insects and birds sang out from all directions. The red crossbills circled around the monster hemlocks on both sides of the stream.

"Good day, gentlemen," Jacob called.

"Hello there. Are you lost?" one of the men said.

"Not really. Enjoying some fresh air."

The old man: "Looks like a rain coming in." A pause. "No fishing poles?"

"Not today. We are brothers, honorably discharged from King George's Army, and we are looking for a haven, on a temporary basis."

"King George's Army?"

Jacob answered, "Yes, sir. Fourth Brigade, Philadelphia."

"Who are you fighting boy?" they started to chuckle.

"Why, American rebels of course."

"And French," says Aaron dejectedly. He sat down and began to pull out the thorns that had caught in his coat.

"I thought you British destroyed them, at New York."

"Yes, well the fight continues, it seems."

The other old man said, "The Americans will win this war…"

"Ha. Impossible, friend." Countered Jacob.

"George Washington from Virginia!"

"A scoundrel."

"He wasn't a scoundrel at Trenton."

His friend said, "And Princeton."

"Fair point." Jacob looked at Aaron with a perplexed look. He whispered, "I thought this was all Tory country?"

"Your friend doesn't say much."

"My brother. Has a bit of the fever."

"And you are seeking safety?"

Jacob said, "Aye. And shelter. Can we buy some food from you, gentlemen?"

"I can get you some salt pork, yes," the fisherman said.

"Much obliged."

"Go to Derr, the German. He sends boys up to Canada to safety! Yes."

"Derr?"

"He sends you Tory boys up to Canada to safety! Yes."

"Splendid. How do we get there?" Jacob asked.

The other old man grunted. "You go to Bakker. Bakker sends you to Derr."

"Bakker?"

"Bakker."

"Where?" Jacob asked, annoyed.

The old men both pointed. "Just right over dem hills. You'll see it!"

That night, they ate boiled rice (salt and butter) with ship biscuit. Jacob tore off a piece of biscuit and chewed like a man possessed.

"Derr. Bakker. Sounds like a Dutch man. Dutch and Germans everywhere!"

"Yes," Aaron said.

"Need a damn German dictionary. Back East, there were mostly Americans!" (A pause) "Are you all right?"

"I'll manage."

"We'll get out of this mess, and pretty soon we'll get you back to that girl of yours. Jane."

"Don't say her name," said Aaron.

"Was she pretty?"

"I don't want to talk about it. Good night." The younger soon fell asleep, thinking of his girl, while Jacob stared straight at the embers of the fire, flipping his long blade over in his hand, thinking of his mother and father and his future. And thinking about the sixteen-year-old boy in that damn prison. What was it Private Tracey? Yes…"

It began to rain.

Three Delaware Indians walked down the road, with leather jackets and beads in their long black hair. Their moccasins left fresh prints on the soft brown trails.

CHAPTER 7

The hills on the faraway horizon looked blue. Spring was coming. The clouds above were formed into dark rounded shapes, like giant horseshoes. There were mud puddles along the side of the road, and a cardinal darted out of some soggy bushes. A few raindrops plunked into the puddles. The only sound the boys heard was a deep hearty *moo* from the cow in the field.

They walked for another hour, and then saw a welcome farmstead sitting dead ahead on a hill.

"This must be where Bakker lives," said Jacob. "Let's go."

Goats grazed in a side field, and behind the house there were many acres of muddy, healthy fields.

They knocked on the door, and soon a friendly man looked at them.

"Good day, how do you do?" Jacob asked, with shoulders back and a confident voice.

"Ha."

"Hello, how do you do?" he said again.

"Ha, hallo." (The man was struggling with the English language...)

"Are you Bakker?"

"Ya, Bakker." The boys wiped their boots and entered. At this point he broke out into some quick Dutch phrases and pointed around at his house, and pointed to the ladies in the room; it was as if he was saying presumably—this is my home and this is my family. It was a house that was rough and aged, but possessed a bit of charm. The first floor contained a parlor and dining room and one bedchamber; upstairs was a small bedroom and an attic/storeroom. The kitchen was a separate structure but attached to

79

the back entryway by a portico. The boys saw, inside the parlor on a tea table, a plate of the miniature round cakes that the Dutch called *koekies* (cookies) beside tiny yellow lilies poking their heads out of a pewter gill. Closer to the window were cut pussy willows in a crock and a pot of green mint. The big hearth was in the dining room.

His wife and daughter were grinding nutmeg into powder, making pies. The kitchen as a result smelled wonderful. There were koekies on a plate.

"You have a handsome home," Aaron said. But they did not answer.

"Remove your hat," Jacob snapped at Aaron. Both men held their hats by their chest.

Jacob got right down to it. "We are from the Jerseys and going to Canada."

"Ya?"

"Canada," Jacob repeated.

The daughter, a girl of maybe twelve, spoke: "You are soldiers from the war?"

"You speak English!"

"A little bit… English," she said, blushing.

"Charming, my dear. Please tell your father—we are going to Canada. Can we purchase snowshoes and fishing poles from him?"

The girl thought…

"Snowshoes and fishing poles?" They repeated. Jacob looked at his brother…

She translated to her parents.

After a minute of fast Dutch phrases and waving of the hands, she said, "We have fishing poles for you. No shoes." The man kept speaking Dutch and looking at the brothers. Sometimes he would chuckle.

After some awkward back and forth, using the girl as a middleman, it was finally arranged after several trying minutes that this Bakker would sell the boys two fishing poles and flint and salt block and a wool scarf, all for eight shillings. They shook hands and smiled.

The transaction being successfully completed, the grown-ups sat down for afternoon tea. Small talk was nearly impossible. The four of them smiled across the table pleasantly. Every so often, they would raise their cups to the others as a "cheers" or "proost"!

Aaron gave the girl a small keepsake, a set of three Indian feathers, probably Seneca, which he found two weeks ago. He pointed to each feather: "Charity, hope, and strength. For you…"

"Thank you, soldier!" she said.

Jacob unfolded his crude map of Pennsylvania and wanted to ask Bakker some final questions. Aaron sat down and smoked his pipe. Mrs. Bakker and the daughter cleared the table and folded the linens.

Bakker pointed down on the creased, yellowed paper and gave the boys a rough idea where they were, which was just off Mahantago Creek, about eight miles east of the river, near the village of Hellerstown (population fourteen or sixteen). All German and Dutch farmers.

Jacob studied the map for a while and turned to his brother and said, "Still about seventy miles to get to Derrstown." There was some pessimism in his voice.

"Mr. Bakker, you know Derrstown?"

"Ha?"

"You know Derrstown, up here?" Jacob pointed.

"Ya. Derr. Ludwig Derr, German man. Ya."

"Splendid, we go there." Jacob said, to no one in particular.

"Ya."

"Yes."

He made a quick comment, and suddenly the three Bakkers started to laugh loudly. Jacob looked questioningly at the daughter. She said, "You will need snowshoes."

"Very funny. Very funny." Jacob sighed…

Bakker was kind enough to let the boys sleep over with the goats in the barn. It was fortuitous too, because that very night a heavy rain fell. Jacob was cleaning his rifle and inspecting the fishing poles. Aaron sat on some straw with his book, and was scribing verses from the Great Book…

April 12, 1778, journal entry:

The LORD is on my side; I will not fear-What can man do unto me? (Psalm 118:6)

Wait on the LORD; be of good courage, and he shall strengthen thine heart—wait I say on the LORD. (Psalm 27:14)

The LORD is my light and my salvation—whom shall I fear? The LORD is the strength of my life—of whom shall I be afraid? (Psalm 27:1)

I will both lay me down in peace and sleep—for thou LORD, only makest me dwell in safety. (Psalm 4:8)

In the morning the boys were off on another trek, due north. They were well rested. As they walked down the hill, heading northwest, they saw several rabbits and a large family of deer.

That afternoon they passed some Indians who rode by on horses. Aaron looked into the eyes of a tough-looking one, and even though they passed in different directions, those tough eyes were locked on poor Aaron until the young man looked away.

They hiked for the next three days. They encountered not another soul.

*****

Around this time, a staff of British military men walked up and down the stairs of the fancy Vine Street house, which was empty and cavernous. The walls were bare, as well as the floors and the mantelpiece—nothing. Nothing but a few scratches and small dents and scraps of newspaper. One of the men smoked and looked out the window. One of them lay down on the floor and put his hat atop his chest and relaxed. The others scratched themselves and chatted. More came in. And then more came in after that.

"You should have seen the lass living here. What an angel!" one of them said. He lifted his hand. "About this tall, looked like a goddess."

"Ah? Where can I find me a lass like that?" They chuckled.

"Take her back to London, and they'd make me colonel!" Laughter.

"Civilized world. Not with these bumbling idiots. Bitches."

They chuckled.

"When you arrive this side of the Atlantic, the women get dumber!"

Laughter. "And homelier."

One of them rubbed the mantelpiece with his dirty fingers and inspected the area. "This is a bloody nice house."

Aye, not every day you see Americans cultivate fine taste in living. Probably had a British builder."

"Yes, sir." Two more soldiers lay down on the floor, put their caps on their chest.

The sergeant said, "Tell that Negro to bring some firewood up here."

"Yes, sir."

Another man, of equal rank, chimed in. "I wouldn't get too comfortable here, sergeant."

"Why the hell not?" he snapped.

"I heard that this Army will once again...relocate. Brands told me he overhead Craig talking to Walker, straight out of headquarters. They said holding Philadelphia affords little advantage. The British Army will march."

"Where?"

"Back to New York City."

There was a collective groan and audible disgust that instantly rose out of the room. The men looked uneasy.

"But there's nothing to do in New York City!" somebody said.

"All the pretty women are here in Philadelphia," they said.

"Well, if I am ordered to leave then I don't got to pay my bloody landlord! Adieu, turkey!"

The sergeant sat up and looked focused. "Brands said this?"

"Aye."

"Well, gentlemen, there's only one thing that we need to focus on. As a unit…"

"What, sergeant?"

"Whiskey, women, and whist! Meet me at Foley's Oyster House tonight at ten. I buy the first round."

"*Yes, sir!*" they called out. A majority of the men left and walked down the stairs. Two remained.

"They should make *me* the commanding general. We would *stay* in bloody Philadelphia!"

They chuckled. He sat back down and covered his face with his black hat.

*****

One damp night at camp, Aaron lay his head down in a coughing fit, and Jacob was out gathering some scraps of wood for the fire. It was dead silent save for the random call of the hoot owl. Aaron closed his eyes and heard the familiar footsteps across the dirt and pine needles, assuming it was his brother. He wanted to sleep, but he was in immense pain all up and down his spine.

"Hello!" an unfamiliar voice called out.

He sat up. "Good day," Aaron said groggily.

"What are you doing out here sick, man? Hunting beaver?" the man was of medium height, close to forty years old. He was holding a long rifle, and he was wearing a wool cap, a brown shirt, and dark pants.

"Looking for medicine. I reckon," Aaron muttered.

"You know what I'm looking for. I am looking for money. You got any?" He pulled out his pistol and pointed it at Aaron. "Give me your money, sick man, or take some lead."

The gunman was joined by what appeared to be his son and an African slave, or servant. They stepped close to the fire and revealed themselves. The Black man had some gunpowder strapped around his neck and was carrying a long blade. The boy, about ten, with dirty blond hair, had an uncomfortable look on his face. He had a long walking stick, about as tall as him.

"Boy, give me your money, or I pull the trigger."

Aaron slowly got up and rifled through some belongings, stalling for time. The three intruders patiently waited. It worked. His brother entered into the scene and hollered, "A lovely evening!"

"What the?" the thief gasped.

"Put your gun down, tough man." He had his pistol locked right on him. Aaron was relieved that Jacob had taken his piece with him on his search for firewood. Nicely done.

The thief staggered. "Now I don't want no trouble…"

"What *do* you want?" Jacob said, penetrating this man's eyes and psyche. He took a step closer.

"I—I just noticed your fire and came in and say hello." The thief smiled uneasily.

Jacob said hello and then pulled the trigger twice and instantly shot and killed the two Caucasian intruders, dead. They fell to the ground nearly simultaneously. Aaron took two steps back quickly, startled.

"You, nigger. Speak up…" said Jacob.

"Yes?" the man nervously uttered.

"What are you all doing out here?"

"That's my master. We going to Duncannon to trade for horses. My master has a business partner—in Duncannon."

"Not good business, trying to rob my brother. He's dead now."

"Yes."

"You're a slave?"

There was no answer.

He turned to Aaron. "There ain't no slaves in Pennsylvania—is it?"

Aaron said, "He is from Baltimore."

"How do you bloody know that?"

Aaron pointed. "The patch on that boy's knapsack. 'Maryland Highlanders.'"

"You from Maryland?" Jacob snapped.

"Yes."

"Are you armed, boy?"

"I have this here sidepiece, but it ain't loaded."

"*Slowly*. Set it down right there," Jacob instructed.

"Yes, sir."

"And that was your master?"

"There. Yes."

Jacob paused, and then spoke, "You're a free nigger now. Go on."

No answer.

"I have nowhere to go," the man said.

Jacob looked at his brother and asked if he was okay. "Yes, fine."

"What's your name?" Jacob asked the visitor.

"I am Potter."

"Maybe he can join us, help us, Jacob?"

"DON'T USE MY NAME, GODDAMN IT. Or I'll shoot you too," Jacob snapped to his brother half-jokingly.

"Right." Aaron rolled his eyes.

"Can you cook?" Jacob asked.

"I can catch fish, mister. And set traps for game."

"Very good. Here's the situation, Potter." Jacob began.

"Yes, sir?"

"My brother and I are headed up north to Canada. And we're moving pretty quick. We left Philadelphia about four months ago. We gotta get first to Derrstown. Do you know where that is?"

"No, I's from Baltimore."

"Can you march fast, and make camp?"

"Yes, sir."

"Like I said before, you are free to choose. You can go on your way, or you can come with us. But if you come with us, let it be known that I am in charge and I call the shots. Understand?"

"Yes, sir."

"My brother is sick, and we have to get up river and get him some medicine. It is not safe down here. I seen some American troublemakers yesterday, and I had to hide in the bushes like some damn fox. Shit. This is my country. Bounty hunters, thieves, rascals. This war is pissing me off. Anyway, I am calling the shots. We are getting outta here and moving fast. North, by north, and then north!"

Jacob spat some tobacco into the fire and said, "And there's a lot of free niggers up in Canada..."

"I will join you."

"Welcome aboard, boy. Do you have a name? Or is it just Potter?"

"You can call me Black Potter."

"Potter. As in, you make pots?" Aaron asked.

"Yes, sir, pots and bowls. Spun from clay and baked."

"Not gonna do us much good out here," Jacob said sharply.

Aaron philosophized. "What's the sense of a good bowl if one has no soup in which to fill it?"

(There were chuckles all around.)

Jacob shot, "You could use it as a helmet—that little dome of yours!" (A chuckle). And he gave his little brother an annoying poke with the butt of his rifle.

Jacob gave some smart orders to his brother and the Black man—for them to strip off any valuables from the dead bodies and, after that, to bury them. Aaron reached into the deceased boy's pocket and found some arrowheads and yarn.

Potter had a bittersweet feeling, burying his master. Forever. "He treated me pretty good."

"Aye?" said Aaron.

"My master before Daniel here, he was a monster. Wish I was burying *him*."

"Well, he may have been pleasant to you, but pulling pistols on me and my brother will get ye into mighty fine trouble. Forget about him."

"Aye." Potter sighed.

Aaron took one of the hatchets from the bodies, and some tobacco. And a newspaper dated May 5, 1778. There was an opinion piece about Scottish immigrants being majority Episcopalian, and not Catholic, as was often presumed. But this form of worship was different to the Presbyterian-dominated lowlands (reading, reading)—and was viewed with suspicion by the authorities. "They, methinks, are second-rate Protestants, and we care very little if highlanders resented that." It was a boring article. Aaron tossed it on the fire.

"You want a smoke, partner?" Aaron offered to Potter.

"Thank you, sir."

"Mr. Jacob says you has a fever, are you sick?" Potter said.

Jacob said, "It's all in his head. He's lovesick! Some angel he met back in the city tore his heart out..."

"Not entirely accurate, brother," Aaron said. "She's waiting for me...to marry her, just as things cool down with this damn rebellion."

"I had a lady once..." Potter sighed. "Eastern shore."

"But I *am* out of sorts. Been coughing and feeling quite ill lately. Do you have any medicine?"

"No, sorry I do not," answered the potter.

*****

Jacob and Aaron and Black Potter next day went up toward Derrstown, straight up north, crisscrossing the Susquehanna, several Lutheran churches, past New Cumberland, McKees Falls, and toward Fort Augusta. They took turns on watch. Potter was a fine companion thus far. Jacob was constantly barking out orders, constantly looking behind them and staying vigilant. At night he was cleaning his guns and keeping an organized eye on the money and valuables and always thinking about Canadian freedom.

On the fourth day, they talked to a farmer who lived next to a lake and asked if he could spare any food for these weary travelers. In return, they helped him repair part of a broken fence. The deal done, the boys enjoyed boiled rice, salt and butter, and some salt pork with ship biscuit.

During this delicious meal, Potter told the boys some stories of the Chesapeake Bay. Of the tasty crabs and the abundance of seafood. And how shipbuilding was a huge industry and how there were lots of jobs in that industry, even for Black men. He also described the brutal heat in the summers, and the presence of ugly jellyfish everywhere.

"Lots of damned Catholics in Maryland," Jacob snapped. "But they were fine soldiers I fought with..."

They slept seven hours behind a shed. They met a group of Germans on the fifth day, and while Aaron and Potter made camp and began cooking, Jacob pumped that European group for any helpful information. Jacob's face was animated. Potter began to drink from his rum cask. Aaron looked half asleep by the smoky fire. They talked for nearly thirty minutes. Aaron enjoyed relaxing and chatting with Potter about seafood, the bay, the crops, and the local politics.

Jacob soon rejoined the group.

"We're going up the Richelieu-Champlain Corridor," Jacob announced. "That German fella been up there twice. He was a part of the Ottawa fur trade."

Aaron and Potter turned and looked at this German.

"I can smell the freedom!" Jacob said, to no one in particular.

"We need a map," Aaron said.

"Give me a smoke," Jacob snapped.

"Does he know how to get to Derr's place?" Aaron asked.

"I didn't ask him that," said Jacob.

"He wasn't one of dem Hessians, was he?" asked Potter.

"I don't think so."

"What was the point of the conversation, brother?"

Jacob switched gears. "You know, I was thinking this morning."

"Yes?"

"What if we sailed to England with Mother and sisters, together? Would father have been proud? Why exactly did we stay back? Why…"

Aaron said, "It took great courage to stay loyal. Tens of thousands of us did. I have no regrets. I think father would be proud. I think he would. What exactly is this concept of America? It's basically Great Britain except they get to tax themselves, and they will be much weaker and have a lot less capital wealth."

A lot less, they agreed.

"They should want stability and government. Instead, they strive for…insurgency and recklessness. I cannot support that!"

Potter said, "Many slaves went to fight for the British. Yes, sir…"

Jacob said, "Yes. The fact that we are fighting each other is…ridiculous. I was shooting and killing my own out there at Germantown…"

"Let's get some sleep," said Aaron.

BEN SCHULZ

They crossed a feeble bridge and came into still more pretty
country. It was late May, and mosquitoes were thick in the evening.
The trio came across a dead man who was tied to a tree and apparently just left tied up. The corpse was getting pulverized with tiny,
noisy insects. They walked right by at a safe distance. No one wanted
to discuss it, but this poor creature was almost certainly a deserter
and fugitive, and that was his punishment. And he was probably
Tory, judging from the once-red uniform that was fading in the sun.
Must stick together. Use good sense.

Despite the discomfort and trekking through the wilds, Jacob
shaved his face every day and stood ramrod straight like a soldier. He
was the picture of strong health. Each stroke of the blade across his
skin made him think of fresh Canadian civilization—money, com-
fort, women, and music. His hair grew long and black, so dirty it was
silklike.

Aaron, in contrast, was struggling. His energy level was sinking
lower, he had stomach issues, and his entire body felt extra warm
and a bit tingly. The only time he moved, it seemed, was when Jacob
would bark out new orders in the mornings.

The hemlocks seemed to accentuate this westward land. They
were everywhere. Around every turn, on every hill, above their heads
pointing at the sun, they shot out of the earth. They spoke, they
danced, they waved, and they slept. Hundreds on the right, hundreds on their left, and thousands for the turkey buzzards to navigate.
Some were 120, some 140, and some 175 feet tall. There were more
hemlocks than people; marking these trees was like counting the par-
ticles of sand on the Jersey seashore.

The dense, lush canopies were like dull green clouds, stretching
as far as the eye could gaze. That faint smell of forest—the pinecones,
the needles, the wet moss—seemed to soak into the trio's clothing.
The air was pure and the breezes invigorating. Jacob, Aaron, and
Potter maintained a distance of fifteen feet between men, and they
trekked.

CHAPTER 8

The way she grinned mischievously when she locked her chamber door. Those dimples, her hair healthy like a field of wheat. The stockings on her small feet. Her movements like a spring breeze, moving her hips and losing herself in passion, happiness, action, togetherness. Squeezing her lover's arms. Her heartbeat getting hotter. Absolute wonder! *Stunning beauty, happy in my company.*

"I want you to forget everything in this crazy world, and just love me, dearly…" she whispered, the breath hot against my face.

After we make love again, she blows some warm air on my cheek. She pulls one of my linen shirts over her naked body.

"Stay with me. Stay with me." She did a little hop and dance and giggle, and a ballerina twist. Laughter. But the laughing grew stone silent and the scene melted away; slowly, instead of vivid colors and a beautiful young lady, there were dark reds and grays and silent laughter and yellow charcoal, and then blackish. And crying. Like several hurt children locked inside a burning barn.

*****

Aaron lifted his head and wiped his mouth and stretched his shoulders. At last, a deep sleep. He felt a stick poking him in the hip. The cold sunlight hit him rudely in the face, beating him like a drum.

"The sun's been up for an hour. Get yourself ready, brother."

From Duncannon the three men hiked due north for several miles, keeping close to the mighty river on their right. The gulls and birds kept them company, and they saw lots of possum and raccoons. They killed three deer near a falls. At times they would pass along tidy farms and see oxen in the field and small cabins up along the rolling green hills.

Rabbits and deer were everywhere. Geese and hawks peppered the sky above. A few days later they saw a crew on a crosscut saw, probably German. May turned to June. The sun was suspended high above like a yellow disc. Jacob heard the thumping of broad axes. A man was fixing his roof shingles. Black Potter caught some walleye and carp, and on one of the nights they enjoyed a nice dinner.

"We are far enough away from Fort Hunter," Jacob announced one evening. "I think we should go to the next available tavern and gather some news."

"What?" Aaron asked, eating the fish.

"Yes. Maybe the war's over! Maybe we'll meet some pretty ladies. Who knows? We need some information, I feel."

"I am not sure that is a good idea," Aaron countered.

"And if they see a Negro, they may string me up!" said Potter.

"I don't think so."

"By the way…this is delicious." He pointed his fork at his plate. Potter smiled.

"Brother—" Aaron began.

"You want to camp out here for the next few months like some damn wild Indians?" Jacob snapped.

"Well, no—"

"They may be looking for my master, Daniel. We murdered them! Seems like a risk don't it?" asked Potter.

"It will be all over the bulletins in every tavern," Aaron said.

"Relax. Nobody knows anybody murdered anybody! He could have fallen in the damn river and disappeared. Wolves coulda got him. Stop acting like a bunch of women." It was a good point.

"And?"

"I want to get to Canada. If we can find a tavern, maybe we can link up with others who want the same thing. We are not the only deserters, brother."

"I wouldn't trust anybody out here and no one at a tavern. It's all spies," Aaron said defiantly.

"You're an old woman," Jacob countered. "What say you, Black man?"

"We gonna need some supplies soon. Maybe Jacob is right. Mighty dangerous though," Potter said.

"Indeed."

"You need to get tougher, Aaron. Stop being so bloody weak!" Jacob's words penetrated rather deep and hurt a bit. Aaron smoked and looked at the fire with a disgusted look.

"How about this. One more week out in these parts, hunting and camping out. And then we find some news, meet some people. We cannot get to Canada like this. I need a damn bath!"

"Sure."

"Same. Getting damn hot out," Potter agreed.

Jacob joked, "All these damn trees are blocking my wind! Did you know there were so many trees in Pennsylvania?"

(A chuckle.) "I think I read that somewhere," Aaron said.

"We can pool our money together, find some horses, maybe a wagon," Jacob said again. "I'm getting bloody tired of running all over these woods."

"Fine. Agreed, brother."

Over the next two days, they scaled back their efforts, and mileage, and decided to just walk for an hour or two, and then enjoy some relaxation. Jacob would hunt possum and deer, Aaron would write stories in his journal, and Black Potter would strike gold along the streams; Carp and walleye were drawn to his worm almost every night.

"Hey, Mr. Aaron, what's the Bible say about fish?" Potter said that night. Aaron referenced Deuteronomy 14:9–10.

"Of all that are in the waters you may eat these: whatever has fins and scales you may eat. And whatever does not have fins and scales you shall not eat. It is unclean for you," he said this with his eyes closed and his head tilted to the sky. He smiled.

Jacob observed, "I wouldn't be surprised if he had that whole book memorized! Reads it all the time…"

One morning, Aaron stripped naked and bathed in the Susquehanna. It was huge and beautiful like a nation all its own. Greenish blue mixed with a touch of brown. Thousands of years, memories. Small whitecaps, wind, fishermen. Indians on both banks.

Canoes. Gulls, osprey. Hawks. Titmouse. Deer. Otter. Muskrats. The water was clean, and he bathed and felt freedom—with the rocks and trees and the menagerie of birds—the thrush and blue jay and gold-finch and more. It was all open out here, no clothes on, wet, natural, alive, light. The cold water tickled. Naked in the river, no one could tell if you were Tory or colonial, British or American, or what your politics. You were just another beautiful animal on the earth. After he dried off, he cut down his long toenails to a suitable length with his little blade. He was hoping the cool splash would subdue his fever, and it did briefly, but it came back. It always did. Unwelcome heat was pulsing through his lungs and joints and skull.

After several more days of walking north, the men came upon a public tavern, off the Post Road at McKee Falls. It was a huge stone structure with a colorful garden off to the left. Long strands of dark ivy clung to the weathered bricks. Several horses, and two carriages, were parked in front. The sweet smoke coming out the top smelled like pork chops glazed with cinnamon. It was a welcome place.

"Remember, you're not a soldier, you're not a deserter. We're mechanics who work down at Swatara Creek. We are here to buy supplies. You do not mention the war, and don't mention your names. Got it?"

"Yes, brother," Aaron answered Jacob.

"What if they ask for my name?"

"Make something up," said Jacob.

They walked in and did not garner much notice. There were about fifteen or twenty folks here, smoking, talking, reading news-papers. A man in the corner was strumming an English guitar. One woman—probably the tavern keeper—was barking instructions to a porter. Potter and Aaron sat by the hearth while Jacob ordered some drinks and inquired for a recent newspaper.

Some men were playing cards and talking of an "iron mine up at Hazelton Mountain." Two large dogs were fast asleep by the fire. Aaron leaned forward, produced a spark, and lit his trusty clay pipe, as Potter sat staring at a faded painting of an ancient chariot race. Up on the ceiling, they had huge eighteen-inch square oak beams that stretched all the way across.

"You think any of these people can help us?" Potter asked, looking around the room with an understated slyness.

"I don't know," said Aaron, blowing thick sweet smoke out, and it slowly thinned and rose to the ceiling.

*****

Meanwhile about, forty miles to the west, over three sets of mountains, some men were talking at the Lutheran church off Lick Run. One of the men talked excitedly about getting a party together and jumping off across the wilds of Pennsylvania and settling out on the western fringes, below Lake Erie, in Venango Country, made famous during the French and Indian War.

"We'll need thirty men, women, children. The opportunities are limitless. We will build schools and businesses. There is a strong trade already established from the lake. We will bring the word of God with us."

"When do you see this happening, William?"

"In one year. One year. The war will be over, and we will head out for new frontiers."

"What if the war is not over in 1779?"

"Are you mad? Cornwallis and Clinton are up on their feet. They are roused. This is the beginning of the end. I give it months…"

Someone else spoke. "This war will open up huge tracts of territory, sir. Western Pennsylvania, the Great Lakes, all the way to the Mississippi. That is what I read last month. Men will be coming over dem mountains."

"Eh?"

"Yes. I met a couple priests from St. Louis here two weeks ago. They are building towns along the Mississippi, sir."

"Quite right," William said.

"What about the Indians?"

"Lord knows," somebody exclaimed.

William said, "Fair point. Shouldn't be a problem along the Venango, but it will be beyond that."

"Let's smoke."

"Yes."

"What do you think of the French entering this grand conflict, William?"

"Shows that the British are bumbling fools. The redcoats should have finished business by Christmas 1776. And they failed. The Americans haven't done a damn thing. It is the British that are giving them hope. And now the French…"

Another said, "Speaking of French, if we head out to Venango next year, we are going to need to *speak* it. That area is filled with those degenerate rascals."

"Why don't they stay in Europe? And Canada?" William joked.

"We'll find a translator, sir."

"Wood can speak some French."

"Wood is an idiot," William said.

"My wife knows a little French!"

"We need hearty folk. Tough. It's going to rain frequently, and it will get exceedingly cold, especially as we get closer to the lake. As many blankets and furs we can carry."

"Yes, William."

"We can *learn* French. We cannot learn strength!"

"It will be so exciting, William!"

William said, "Splendid." A pause. "Do you realize that England and France…have been fighting…for one hundred years nearly? Sixteen eighty-eight. Sixteen ninety. All over Europe and America. They hate each other. Do you realize that our grandchildren will live in a settled territory with relative peace? Think about that."

"England or France as rulers?"

"I don't know. Maybe France," William said.

"So long as they don't turn us into damn Catholics, friend."

"I'll drink to that," William said, winking.

The men and women lifted their glasses and toasted to a planned westward expedition to Venango Creek for 1779…

"To Venango!"

*****

Jacob Abbot hurried back to the hearth. He weaved around the man with the guitar and hurriedly unfolded the newspaper.

"Where are the drinks?" Potter asked.

"She is bringing them over," said Jacob. "Lot of ugly women here!" He eyed the text and pointed to the most interesting headlines. "Look here. Howe is out, Henry Clinton is in. Good Lord."

"Howe is a fool," Aaron said. "Poor communicator. He left Burgoyne out to dry and lost thousands of good troops. For what? So he could dillydally!"

"No argument here. Clinton is not a fool. He will fight and end it! You'll be back in Jersey with that girl of yours before you know it!" He slapped Aaron hard on the back.

The tavern keeper set down some ales, and some tea for Aaron. Jacob told her, "That is Peter. Peter don't drink."

The lady gave "Peter" a wink. "That's fine. Tea is good for you, love."

"Yes, ma'am." She walked away.

"Peter?" Aaron checked with his brother sarcastically.

"You look like a Peter. Peter from the West Indies! Doesn't he look like a Peter?"

"Sure," Potter said.

Black Potter, who could hardly read, looked at the price of eggs in the newspaper and was appalled. "*Six* shillings a dozen! This war is tearing the country up!"

"Yes, sir. Sit up straight, Peter!"

One of the locals came over to the trio and asked them if they knew of any work to be had. They said they didn't know, that they were from Swatara Creek. They had a smoke with the man.

"Do you know anyone with a wagon service, who takes trips to Canada or Lake Erie?"

"Nah, I reckon I do not. But I can find some good horses for ye!"

"Not right now." Jacob looked at the newspaper and drank his beer...

"Who is Lafayette?"

The stranger said, "Some kind of knight I suppose..."

Lafayette. A marquis. (They had trouble pronouncing it...)

"*MarKEE.*"

"*Maakwey.*"

"And he is fighting with the rebels?"

The stranger said, "Aye. Figured the French would get involved. Embarrassed twenty years ago, and they are back. Save face. Degenerates!"

"Degenerates."

"A valued officer for General Washington. Quite wealthy, it seems," the man said.

"Who cares?"

"And he's about your age, Peter," said Jacob.

"Don't call me that," Aaron said. The stranger said bye and walked back to the bar area.

Suddenly Aaron caught a paragraph and snatched the paper all to himself. "The British have left Philadelphia," he read.

"The British have left Philadelphia, gentlemen. Let's go back home, brother!"

"No."

"Yes!" Aaron shouted.

"No, brother. Hold on—"

"I can find Jane."

"Too dangerous! Relax, dammit," Jacob said.

"The British are gone, heading to New York. They are not even looking for us anymore!"

"No!"

"Keep your voice down," Potter said sternly.

"Our homes are back there. And Jane! It is wide open. What is the hesitation?" Aaron shouted.

Jacob got into his face. "We are deserters. On the run. Just because the British have left Philadelphia, don't mean they have *cleared out* of bloody Pennsylvania! You out of your head? You have a price on your head. That hasn't changed. Even a damn American can bag us. You're not bloody safe. Relax."

"But—"

"Relax. And what if you got back to Philadelphia! You're just going to find a job and place to live, and settle in? During this war?

You're a Tory. Doors slammed in your face. And Jane probably went to New York too for her safety..."

"Rubbish. So you'd rather stay out here with the raccoons and deer, sleeping in the leaves? Christ."

Jacob grabbed him by the arm. "Keep your voice down. I am your older brother. And I'm in charge of this operation. Mother would want you to stay safe. I'm taking you to Canada. We will wait out the war and head back home. I promise, brother. We've made progress already."

"I don't know if this is progress!" Potter said.

"Shut up, Black man," snapped Jacob.

Aaron ripped his arm free. "Our family belongs on the East Coast, not out here! The way Father arranged. And you are pulling us from that."

"The family's gone, the war scattered us..."

"Keep your voices down," Potter snapped. Others at the tavern were looking over in their direction because of the commotion and arguing. It was safe to say their cover was blown.

"Our family needs to be at Somerset!"

"What family? We are at war. Do you want to get killed? Do you know how many American bandits are on the path between here and the sea? Jane is gone. The British are gone. You need to stay here with me. You are safe! How do you know our house is still there? They burnt it. They destroyed that region! This is war. Your life before 1776 is over!" Jacob yelled.

"Keep your voices down. We are simple mechanics, remember?" Potter said.

Aaron leaped at his brother, and they began to fight and wrestle. Potter tried to split them up. Glasses broke, and a tiled creamware bowl fell and broke. The tavern keeper yelled at them. A dog started barking. People stood up and gasped, smiled, and cheered. Jacob had his brother around the neck. Aaron was kicking him in the leg and shin. Potter had Jacob by the shoulders, but Jacob was strong enough to keep both men in check, hit on his brother, while at the same time telling anyone who would listen to "calm down." Calm down. Another glass rolled off the oak table and crashed on the stone floor.

One of the employees yelled at them, and somebody threw a knife at them and told them to stop it and be quiet!

Soon, they were able to calm Aaron down. "Sit! Relax. Sit your ass down!"

"It's okay. We're brothers." Jacob smiled.

"Sorry, everybody, we're brothers." Some people chuckled.

"This is Peter from the West Indies," Jacob said, to more chuckles at the bar. Like a big brother, he was playfully slapping Aaron's cheek with a devilish grin.

"Shut up, Jacob," his brother said.

Jacob calmly approached a large, muscular patron who had a blue knit cap, and he handed him the utensil that had very recently been thrown. "Here. You throw anything at me again, Fat Guts, I will shove it in your asshole." The man and his friends quietly looked at him with surprise. Inaction was the wise course here; some men (the elder Abbott) best be left alone.

The men drank their drinks and had another round, and they paid for some peas and onions in cream sauce with chunks of salty ham. They saw some British officers come in around 9:00 p.m., and they quietly walked out. Jacob paid the bill because he had the valuable Spanish coins in his purse. Potter and Aaron watched the transaction and began to miss dealing with civilization back east. Currency, consumerism, economics—none of these things mattered the last several weeks. They had failed to find anybody who could rent them a wagon or some horses, but the entire venture was not wasted for sure—they enjoyed the buttery corn, the drinks, and the recent news back east. All the same, Jacob was not happy. The prospects of Canada were no better than they were twelve hours ago. Outside, the smell of fresh horse dung. Aaron looked up for a chance to see Leo, but the dark sky was shrouded with clouds.

The men walked for another day, across a barren prairie where they saw twenty or thirty playful deer and clusters of purple mint. They climbed over another angled ridge and took a break in the forest. Jacob and Potter broke a nice sweat, but Aaron was feverish and shaky. His fever inched up higher. He wanted to trade in everything, his future, his tomorrows, his prospects, everything, to spend just one hour with Jane.

He had had enough of the drooping hemlocks and the tough, rubbery venison, in this place that had no name. He dabbed his forehead, wiped down his muddy boots with a damp cloth, and picked thorns and thistles out of his breeches. He built a fire, every so often coughing and spitting some gunk from his lungs into the dead leaves on the dirty ground.

*****

Black Potter crossed over a creek bed and looked to his left. He made sure he was loaded. Cocked. Two blue jays danced across the sky. It was early June. Jacob and Potter were looking for wild game, but all they came across were insects and birds. He wiped his forehead and then dried his hand on his trousers. He looked to the right and then to the left. He dug in his toes and steadied himself, this man from Baltimore.

There is never a good time for a murder, and for Aaron's circumstances, it could not get any worse. The way he was feeling, it may have been better in fact if he—Aaron—were killed. The afternoon began just like the previous dozen or so—two men go out for a hunt, while the third man keeps camp and prepares for supper. On this day, Aaron played camp hand, washing utensils, polishing tools and guns, building a tall fire, and generally keeping a lookout for any strangeness lurking about the periphery. He found out about the murder hours after it happened; most gunshots in the late afternoon, it was assumed, was aimed at potential supper—boar, deer, rabbit, et al. He heard two loud shots, about one-fourth mile distance to the east.

He shot Jacob Abbot in the chest—BANG!—and then he casually walked up to the bleeding man and stuck a knife into his neck, six inches deep. Killed dead. Jacob never made a sound. Potter next did the deed that he set out to do, which was empty the victim's pockets of any and all valuables, especially the stained leather pouch fastened inside the brown waistcoat. Spanish silver, extra powder, hunting knife, a flint, and a pinkish kerchief. And of course, he grabbed the rifle off the mud. Black Potter fled to the west quickly and quietly. Murdered.

*****

Jacob Abbot 1754–1778. That was what the sign on the crudely made cross said. Aaron was exhausted and defeated, too tired to shed tears. Sometimes man is pushed too far down in the muck to show any emotion. But he had the strength to bury his brother out here—where exactly?—and spoke a few words of prayer.

Thessalonians 4:14: For since we believe that Jesus died and rose again, even so, through Jesus, God will bring with him those who have fallen asleep.

A fine man, a great man, a leader. This was an act of treachery. But this was war—even though the party was adrift miles into the backwoods of actual combat, that didn't mean the war was not directly over their heads like dark weather, like toxic air, like oxygen, like Leo up there, who was no longer smiling and dancing, but instead still and lifeless.

Aaron whacked the cross into the earth a couple times with the butt end of his knife. Rest in peace. He had lost a father, and now a brother. Brave men. Are they reconnected now? He sat at the camp, alone, and looked at the fire. No more fathers, no more brothers. Fire was about all he had left, until of course the rain would come. He didn't think of anything; he was numb, inanimate. Blank. The raccoons came by and kept going. Even they could tell the morale at this camp was ice-cold sadness. The fire burned hot. It was midnight. June 1778. Perhaps the middle of the month, but what did it matter. He was about five miles from Hummel Farm, on the west bank of the Susquehanna, just south of Fort Augusta. He had come 160 miles. Into the forest. And now he sat. alone.

Send thee help from the sanctuary…he is brought down and fallen. But we are risen and stand upright. Save, Lord, let the king hear us when we call…

After a couple hours' sleep, he sat up and nibbled on some jerky. He felt terrible. Luckily it hadn't rained. He began to think positive thoughts and the possibility of luck, of new opportunities. His body was still in shock and had not succumbed to the full mourning period; he was in transition perhaps. Maybe he could go back to the British service—at least they had bread and water and beans, and tea. And there would be companionship. But then he felt defeated and exhausted. It was delirium perhaps. He couldn't see himself taking ten steps; how could he get to Canada? Or New Jersey? Or to any civilization whatever? He needed some medicine. His mind was spinning, and it made him sicker. *Should have never left Philadelphia—my love, my job, my health, my life was there. There.* He coughed, his body felt hot and weak.

Aaron decided to update his journal: *My god. I believe even Job would lose his patience to be in my circumstances.*

The next day it rained. He wiped a tear from his face, thinking about his older brother. He checked his pouch and satchel and confirmed that no, he had no hard currency, that Jacob had handled the money. Which direction would he venture? The millions of spruce, fir, hemlocks, maples, and oak made him feel claustrophobic. Which direction was the right one?

CHAPTER 9

Meanwhile, back in Philadelphia, a fierce gust of wind blew hard west to east, Eighth to Fifth to Third Streets and over the Delaware. The horses in the city braced themselves. Debris, grass, dirt, and dust flew through the air. The hanging sign in front of the hatter was swinging back and forth, back and forth, making little squeaky noises. Another trash barrel banged into the side of the customs house. There was a copy of *Institutes of Natural and Revealed Religion* (1772–74) by Priestley that slid across the street and stuck to the one of the coffee shops. A regular postman walked sideways through the wind, lugging his huge sack of letters and small packages; every few seconds he had to hold onto his tricorn firmly with his hand. This was a tough day, because of the elements. He dropped off at 500 block at Vine street and at 490, 470, and 440. His sack was getting somewhat lighter by now. He found the opening at the door and tossed the letter inside, and quickly moved on to the next house. The letter said, *Jane Canterbury*

And there it landed, with about eleven others that looked almost identical.

Jane Canterbury, Jane Canterbury, Jane Canterbury, Jane Canterbury

The handwriting was from the same sender. Some of the envelopes were sharp and mint, some were bent and soiled. Identical handwriting.

Nobody opened these, and nobody saw these; nay, a local cat saw them! Sometimes it would bend in and sniff them. The beautiful house, with so many happy memories, sat empty. Cobwebs had formed along the shadowy crevices along the mantlepiece and most corners of the dusty rooms.

Jane Canterbury would never see the letters. She would never see Philadelphia again either. She spent all her time now, talking to the angels and other creatures that flew around her room in the insane asylum. North Carolina. She laughed, wept, and stared blankly all day at nothing at all. Sometimes she stared out the window or straight at the white stone wall. She thought about the opium and pain and intensive treatment after she lost her man, got beaten by Tayloe, lost her money, and ended up in the Carolinas, alone. She wore a cross around her neck and told people she was a bishop. She waved the cross around and told her empty room that she was saving those troops, officers, killers, bastards. It's okay because she was saving them. She laughed. But then she thought about the opium and turned quiet. Did it save her? Did it mask the pain and dull the anguish of the last eight weeks? The beating from Tayloe, the abuse of redcoats after that, the hitting, the beating, the many sexual violations that were now a part of her, baked into her. And she used to forget. Now it was harder to forget. Family would try to visit her, but she didn't recognize them, or just didn't care. When someone mentioned Aaron Abbott, she laughed and held tight onto the cross. When someone mentioned Philadelphia, she looked confused. Most nights she lay on her wooden cot, and sucked on her nightgown like it was candy, and stared at the ceiling. She was monitored closely by the medical staff at the ward. Their diagnosis was *depression, mania or psychosis, substance abuse, insomnia, and delirium—in a general sense,* insanity.

*****

General Sullivan looked at Major Bowman, Captain Helms, and Captain Clark.

"Show me the block house on the map."

"There, sir." One of the men pointed.

"Right." A pause. "These are the magazines?"

"Those are the powder magazines, sir."

"Aye. Where did you get this, soldier?"

"The Spanish merchant from St. Louis," he answered.

"Father Bartolome?" the general asked.

"Yes, sir."

"Did he demand compensation?"

"Yes."

"And?"

"The matter is with Congress currently, sir."

"Excellent. Well done. We'll all be long dead be the time he gets a response," the general quipped.

Chuckles filled the room.

"Right." General Sullivan looked up from the map, to about fourteen serious faces inside a crude cabin. He stood in one corner, black boots, a wool coat with a collar and cuffs, a hat that was generally turned up on the side, a linen shirt, a red vest, and Navy breeches.

"Gentlemen, this expedition will reap major benefits to our American cause. I thank you in advance for your service and steady efforts. Pennsylvania is our state and not Britain's, and certainly not the Indians'. As you know, there are treaties proposed and pending as we speak, to clear this area of Seneca and Delaware and the rest of them. *This is American country.* General Washington will win the war out east and I—you and I together—will win the war out west. Am I clear?"

"*Yessir!*"

"And not only Pennsylvania. Western New York, the Great Lakes, the Ohio River Valley. Gentlemen, this land is ours. It used to be British, but no longer! I have assembled 130 men to make it so. Fine men, well trained. We come across British troops, we demand their surrender, or we kill them. We come across Seneca and Delaware and Iroquois, we demand they align with us and our mission, or we tomahawk them. All of them. This is war. This is our land. Congress has given us their approval. Washington has given his blessing and signature. We have been furnished with every necessary I wanted. There are no excuses. Not manpower, not the weather, not Congress, nothing. We are not outnumbered. We have the advantage. Address your squad tonight. We march at sunrise tomorrow. I aim to be at Fort Augusta by the end of one week. Colonel McIntosh will be expecting us. Go, gentlemen. Go."

"*Yes, sir!*" The room cleared out, leaving only Bowman and Helms.

Helms complained, "We have had a fatiguing journey to the north bank of the river. Much distressed by the Indians."

"A damn set of villains, sir," Bowman agreed.

"Methinks there are still Indians that await our march, sir," Helms said. He spoke with a stutter, and his body emitted raw fear.

"Probably right. It's the fate of war. A good soldier never ought to be afraid. Am I clear?"

"Yes, sir."

"The only probable chance of safety is…"

"Sir?" Helms asked.

"Using good sense."

Helms spoke quickly and nervously. "Yes, sir. We met a priest from Canada last week. He said he saw dozens of dead bodies all through western New York and parts north of here. Slaughtered. The Seneca and Iroquois, they give no quarter. French, American—matters not. They ordered the prisoners to be tomahawked. Or tortured."

"I believe it. I don't plan on getting captured. Do you, Captain?" said Bowman.

"No, sir," said Helms.

"Very good. Dismissed."

*****

The dysentery had done its worst. He had trouble swallowing. The small campfire burned out, and once again Aaron was surrounded by chilly dampness, even though it was July. The night before he had forced down some berries and morsels of Indian hoecake, but he spent most of the night spitting it all back up, along with some blood and bile for good measure. He could remember when he stood at a healthy 135 pounds, but today he was at a skeletal 103 or 104. He had a fever and had nothing (aside from that). It's not often where a man's internal temperature was greater than his weight on the scales. He had nobody except for his enormous captors, the hemlocks. They had him. He was outnumbered by the state tree of Pennsylvania at 6.4 million of them, to one of him. He could not outrun them because he could not stand. In a mocking fury the hemlocks—the demons—only grew taller at 300 feet, and thicker and more arrogant. They had won. Very soon they would have themselves another dead victim, and their forest floor—their stomach—would digest his mangled remains, along with the animal carcasses and insects, bark, bird brains, moss and soggy leaves, and billions of tons of mud, all of it cooked up and fossilized, swallowed, and a part of history wiped clean off the earth, forever. And no human would record it or remark it. The hemlocks looked down at this pathetic Tory soldier just as a man slams down his silvery ax upon a pinned-down rooster. Let it come already. The hemlocks won. They grow and wave and shine bluish green like a proud nation. About 6.4 million, bigger and stronger than any nightmare Aaron could remember.

He summoned the strength to locate a pencil and his journal, and he wanted dearly to write a letter to Jane, which would serve as love letter-cum-SOS-cum-suicide note. He was alone. This was the end of the rope. He was washed over and ice cold and thoroughly beaten down. It had been many weeks since he encountered another human; all he saw were trees and rocks and rain, billions and billions of bloody trees staring at him. He felt too weak to open up the journal, so it just rested lifeless in his cold and clammy hands. Maybe he would wet his pants again; at least that kept him warm for a while. Let it come already. The hemlocks won.

Another day and another, a week probably. Aaron lay on the earth with his eyes open. One night a huge bear stepped into his camp with crashing footsteps. It was near eight hundred pounds with long killer claws. He lifted his head and sniffed the surroundings and began to lick the side of a tree. He looked right at Aaron. Aaron's head didn't move off the mud, but even so their eyes met. *End me. Take me.* The bear stepped on the journal and stepped past some vomit, and then roared. He explored the sick man's pack with his snout—he probably smelled remnants of beef jerky or spilled nutmeg. He roared again. *End me. Take me. Honorable death. Honorable death. Let it come already. The hemlocks won.*

The beast sniffed Aaron's body. He could feel the strange breaths at the side of his face, and he closed his eyes. But it wasn't to be. The bear sauntered out of the camp with an air of unfulfillment, the twigs and leaves cracking and popping under the enormous frame.

Jacob. Mother. Dear sisters. Any and all future lovers and friends and family, and enemies. Jane, that smile and wavy hair and sunny demeanor, she is no doubt living a great life in London or Paris at this point, holding a sun umbrella and giggling. And to Father—a true hero—it was time to go. They would understand! We tried the best we could. I came out here, 133 miles from—wherever. Aaron closed his eyes and awaited death. *They would understand...*

*****

"What is it?" yelled Bowman. Three Navy-coated officers entered with fresh dispatches.

"News of a battle out east, sir. Clinton's Army marching through New Jersey." Bowman snatched a letter from his lieutenant. He read with wild and excited eyes, flying across every line of text.

"*Monmouth Courthouse...*" he read. Silence for thirty seconds. Bowman handed the missive back to Helms.

"Ten thousand men on his way to New York. I told you he would leave Philadelphia. Again. I told you he would leave Philadelphia."

"Yes, sir."

"He wanted to move all them damn loyalists out to sea." A pause.

"We had them, gentlemen. Almost had them." He knocked his desk with his fist. "Sounds like Charles Lee lost his nerve at the wrong time. What does it say to you?"

"I came to that conclusion as well, sir," said Helms.

Bowman walked over and looked out his window.

"We may have lost Monmouth, but history will show it as a great draw between two evenly matched armies. Washington is in a good spot. A good spot. He will lock down New Jersey. Clinton will stay right where he is."

"How do you know he is going to New York, sir?" Helms asked.

"Money. Safety. British influence. New York is the key to the whole continent."

"Quite right."

"I know Clinton. He needs His Majesty's Navy right at his back, at all times. Feels naked without them!"

"Yes, sir. And Washington?"

"Washington has Philadelphia and New Jersey, and his job now is to make sure Clinton stays in New York."

Bowman looked at Helms and changed his tone. "As a result, the fighting of this entire war...will shift to other locations."

"Where?"

Bowman thought for a moment. "Wherever the British want to go," he said, followed by nervous laughter.

"Yes, sir." A pause.

Just then, another soldier knocked on the door. *Knock, knock.*

"Enter!" yelled Bowman.

"Sir."

"What is it?"

"We have taken another prisoner, sir, this morning."

"Who is he?" Even though he was talking, Bowman was also reading and initialing random dispatches. He circled a name *Captain Pipe* (Hopocan) on his sheet.

The man said, "He appears to be a Tory or a trapper. Perhaps lost. He is in mighty bad shape. Skin and bones, this one."

"Tomahawk him if he's a Tory," he said, laughing.

"And if he's a simple trapper?"

"Then give him something to eat and tell him to go away! I shouldn't have to tell you this," said Bowman.

"Yes, sir."

"How many times do I have to *repeat myself! Any man who hasn't the zeal and attachment to the American cause, eliminate them!*"

"Yes, sir." The man disappeared and slammed the door. Bowman made a few notes on the dispatches in front of him. He read letters from Congress. A letter from General Sullivan. Studied the map of Fort Augusta and the map of Fort Pitt. He read again the profiles of White Eyes, *Captain Pipe* (Hopocan), and John Kill Buck (Gelelemend). "Damn set of villains."

He thought more about Monmouth Courthouse. Washington was doing well. Outnumbered and outgunned, for three years running. Clinton was now bottled up. And what next? He looked out the window and saw several men tugging a wagon through some soupy mud; one American officer was barking encouragement. Two mules stood in the mud and watched the efforts. Another man was fixing his bayonet onto his Brown Bess; another man was drinking coffee and laughing. His friend was spitting into a blazing orange fire. One man adjusted himself and was talking about...something. The Indians across the road were cooking some trout in a skillet. Another Indian was wiping down his fine leather saddle with a damp cloth. Bowman had fine men. Fine men. He took a nice long breath and just then realized what would happen next. His face changed, and he looked at the wood floor. The fighting will certainly shift to the Carolinas. The South!

Collapsed in the mud, lots of chatter and soldiers and Indians and activity that went right by. A huge wagon sat up on the hill. He smelled cabbage and corn and potatoes and gruel. Soft wind, no stars. Cold mud. *Slap. Slap.*

A tall, dirty officer in dark blue stood over Aaron and began slapping him roughly in the face. "Wake up, boy! *Wake* up!"

"Yes?" he said quietly...

"What are you doing out here? You a Tory?" the man in the Navy coat yelled.

"No, sir." Aaron tried to sit up but could not; the muscles and machinery in his body simply wouldn't allow it.

"You look like a damn Tory to me."

"And he smells like a Tory," he said, chuckling. The officers looked at each other with a smirk...

Aaron began to speak...

"What?" the men asked.

"I am a simple trapper. I live near Swatara Creek. My brother was killed. Please help me."

"Why should I help you?"

"I need medicine."

"Who killed your brother?"

Aaron thought a moment. "A damned British deserter. A villain."

"He's lying. He's a Tory."

"I'm not a Tory," grunted the soldier, eyes still closed.

"Boy, if you are a Tory, I am going to tomahawk your red-coated ass."

"I am not a Tory. My father fought with…"

"What?"

"My father fought with…" But Aaron was about to nod off.

The officer barked, "Put him on the wagon with the others, get him to the fort. You caught me in a generous mood, trapper."

"Obliged, sir," Aaron whispered, his eyes shut. He heard boots stepping around him in the mud.

"Get him some brandy and water."

"Yes, sir."

The officer had taken a few steps but then stopped, turned in the mud, and took a step toward Aaron. "And if I find out you're a damn Tory, I will personally go down to Swatara Creek and burn your damn house down and roger your mum. Sideways," he said, chuckling.

"Do you *hear* me?"

There was no answer. The officer walked away. And so the sergeant stepped in and barked, "Grab his feet, get him on the cart. Shouldn't be too hard—this boy is a hollow tree branch. It looks like he confused his breeches for the bloody privy. That damn smell!"

There were some chuckles.

One of the men are taken aback. "This man is on fire! What a fever! You touch him."

"No, you bloody touch him. He's not getting me sick. There's shit and grease all over him!"

"Was he living under ground?" one of the troops wondered.

"Christ…"

"Feel how hot he is!"

Aaron opened his eyes slowly.

"Help me!" said the soldier. He was barely conscious and breathing intermittently.

"I rank you, sergeant. *Grab that hollowed trapper and throw him on the fucking cart!*" he yelled.

"Yes, sir."

A strong sergeant in a Navy coat grabbed his boots and helped his partner, who had Aaron's shoulders and underarms.

The sergeant muttered to his partner, "Likely won't matter. This boy will be dead by supper!"

The men picked up the sick man and tossed him. Aaron was jolted with a thud and landed in his own sick, in his crotch and pants; he felt like his body was being raked over coals. He felt his teeth were dangling out of his head, his fingers and toes icicles, and his spinal column was cold soup. Mostly, he was damned tired.

They gave him some bread and a shot of brandy. Aaron could live another day. There was a mass of random bodies in the wagon. Indians. Some elderly. Trappers. Free Blacks. Maybe sixteen or eighteen. It was like a big hospital cart. The wagon inside stunk something fierce, like one hundred dead animals under a cloth blanket.

Up ahead a man cracked his whip, and then the strong wooden wheels turned in the mud. They were headed to the fort.

CHAPTER 10

There was a cloaked minister who walked up and down the dark corridor at the hospital wing of the fort, visited the sick beds, and provided encouragement and felt the boys' foreheads with the back of his hand.

"Lord be with you," he said.

"Lord be with you," he said.

Aaron was propped up in bed. His hair was slicked back with grime and moisture. His eyes were extremely tired and felt puffy. It felt like there was some food in his gut, although he didn't recall ever eating. His head was spinning, and lots of medicine was surging through his body. He also felt like he had been asleep for about fifteen hours!

Most of the boys here, up and down the hall, were fast asleep. Knocked out. Beaten.

"Lord be with you," he said

"Father," Aaron acknowledged quietly, a nod of the head.

Aaron watched the old man, dumbly—with white hair and stooped shoulders and black cloak, talking to all the boys; if the boy happened to be asleep, the man passed by. Most of the patients lay motionless and flashed an appreciative smile. But a few boys had trouble doing even this—maybe it was the shell shock, the depression, the massive brain injury, the fear or the hell or the terror they saw against the Mohawk Indians, or the utter defeat and devastation. And they did not smile; they looked at the minister and simply wondered who they were and what they were doing here. What was their name?

Outside, some Indians sold the fort some goods, medicinal plants, and herbs like snake root. They had cord and rope in their hands. An officer handed them a sack of goods, which acted as compensation. Chuckles, salutations. Some of the patients saw scenes like this when they were at mess, and they could look out the windows.

Aaron passed the time by reading his Bible and updating his journal—one of the last entries, in a shaky hand, was *nauseous, high fever. Please come, Jane. I need you. Jacob dead. No family. No country. Misery. 1778.*

He shut the book. He slept for three more hours. He had a powerful and strangely vivid dream of a skulk of foxes, who were sailing a formidable ship of the line, 173 feet long, crashing over waves, rocking as a giant beast. The foxes gathered in a wide circle above decks, and they all held hands. Sometimes they would bark and howl and sing. The foxes smiled. The waves would crash over the rails and soak some of the foxes, but they never let go of their partners' hands, never stopped barking and howling and smiling. The white canvas sails snapped and jerked in the wind. The main sail, upon closer inspection, was an image of a fox. In this dream, one of the foxes broke the fourth wall and spoke: "Soldier. Soldier…"

"Soldier. Soldier," said the doctor. "Hello!"

Aaron opened his eyes. "Hello, doctor."

And then the doctor leaned in. "I am Doctor Wilkerson." A pause. "Who is Jane Canterbury?"

"I will make her…my wife," the patient muttered sadly. "Why?"

"You were moaning her name all night. Sweaty beast! We changed your sheets three times…"

"Fever?" Aaron wondered.

"Aye, soldier. And vomiting," said the doc.

"Did you bleed me?"

"No, not yet. Some salts and Peruvian bark. We'll see if there's progress." The doctor turned and spoke to a colleague, "Give that man some potash nitrate, right now."

"Yes, sir."

The doctor wrote something on his papers. "How much did you weigh back home?"

"One thirty," Aaron muttered.

"Good Lord," he said, looking at his papers that said *ninety-seven*. "From Philadelphia?"

"Yes, sir."

"A Tory soldier?"

"No, sir."

The doctor shot him a quick look to try to decipher the truth. "No, sir," he repeated.

"Have I lost weight?"

"Yes, pilgrim," said the doc.

"The war still going on?"

The doctor motioned to all the hospital beds with sick and dying men in uniform. He said, "What do you think?"

"Doc, do you know pray tell what is the date?" Aaron muttered.

"Aye. It is the eleventh of July."

"Do you know where Jane Canterbury is, Doc?" Aaron asked, rather pathetically.

"No, pilgrim. Say…"

"Yes?"

"What are you doing out here at the fort?"

"I don't know," said Aaron.

The doctor stared at Aaron with an inquisitive look, before scribbling something on his little medical notebook.

*****

If all went as planned, signers of the treaty were to be White Eyes, Captain Pipe (Hopocan), and John Kill Buck (Gelelemend) for the Lenape, and Andrew Lewis and Thomas Lewis for the Americans. Witnesses included Brigadier General Lachlan McIntosh, Colonel Daniel Brodhead, and Colonel William Crawford.

Clark, Helms, Bowman, McIntosh, and the men marched about thirty-three miles and rendezvoused with the Americans Brodhead and Crawford and their circle. They shook hands and had a smoke, and went over the details of the upcoming objectives and goals and the ceremonies planned at Fort Pitt. They had a conference for ninety minutes, where most everything was worked out. And then, like gentlemen officers of a high rank and advanced station, they proceeded to open up several bottles of liquor and sat down to a sumptuous meal of lamb, veal, corn, and vegetables.

Crawford was a proud man and a great talker. He could hold a crowd's attention with his deep military cadence, rhythm of speech, and sense of humor. Born in 1722, he marched with Braddock in the French and Indian war, and he knew the Fort Pitt area very well; he had built a cabin and settled just east of there. He looked at all the troops, had (another) quick shot of whiskey, and boomed, "Did you hear about the Russian Cossack engineer working along the Volga River? There was this fancy prince who wanted to build a new cottage for himself and his beautiful wife. Over several days, they were scouting out the perfect location along the Volga River. His wife said to him, we need plenty of sunlight for my vegetables to grow! We need good soil and flat earth for my horses to roam and be happy! Finally, they found a great spot. The prince hired a team of Russian Cossack builders and architects—the best in Russia. They started construction, and the prince and his wife were so happy. After three years, the Russian Cossacks finished—it was a stunning thirty-room villa with a domed roof made of marble. And then the prince and his wife came to view this achievement. They arrived and the Cossacks stood with pride. But unfortunately, the man's wife said, I don't like it. I want my cottage to be on the *other* side of the Volga. Tear this down and start again, over there." There were light chuckles. "She was pointing to the opposite bank, about a mile away. The royals left, and the Cossack builders were feeling depressed. What shall we do? What shall we do? And then, the main Russian Cossack had a great idea. He grabbed a shovel, walked several paces behind the cottage, and started digging. Some of his men said, what are you doing, Dmitri? Why are you digging back there? And this man Dmitri looked up to them and said, 'Don't you get it? We don't need to move the cottage. We simply need to 'move' the river...'"

Loud and raw laughter bellowed out around the table. Even the teller of the tale was laughing uproariously, slapping the back of his buddy seated to his left. This went on for ten or fifteen seconds and then died down.

Over four months' time, Aaron got back to stable, decent health. They had him eating eggs and ripe tomatoes and drinking lots of herbal tea and going for walks around the fort. This was Fort Augusta, one of the westernmost Pennsylvania forts built just before the war, he was informed. He was about 117 pounds. They had him do some sitting-up exercises and punching a mattress, to monitor his stamina. They had him squat and rise, squat and rise. During these many weeks, he had shown the authorities he could keep food down, he did not have a fever, and he was just about ready to step out beyond those iron gates, into the wilds of central Pennsylvania. Jane meanwhile did not answer his letters. None of them.

Thankfully, they brought him his little pack of belongings, found near his firepit with the giant footprints of the grizzly. There was his Bible, correspondence and notes, medicine, knickknacks, and his long blades and sidepiece. It was late autumn and getting chilly outside.

Dr. Wilkerson shook Aaron's hand. "Good luck, pilgrim. Get out of here."

Aaron signed some papers down the hall and recognized one of the American officers near the gates as he departed. His waistline had shrunk two inches, and so he and the nurses had tightened a cord around his waist to keep his breeches up and secure. They had offered to cut his long greasy hair, but he politely declined because, he said, he wanted to look like his older brother.

"Sir, permit me to take this moment and say thank you for taking me in and getting me the proper treatment to conceivably—"

"Abbott?"

"Yes, sir."

The man, remembering the boy and how everybody assumed he was a sick and injured *Tory*, turned a bit harsh. "Get out of my goddamn sight. Start marching, boy."

"Yes, sir."

A man name Sam was hired as a temporary guide to head with Aaron toward Chambers Gate. The roads were hard to come by, as this was thick wilderness to points west and eventually—hopefully—north to Canada. Aaron stepped outside the gates and squinted in the cool sun; his legs stood with gratitude and at the same time hesitation. The earth felt right under his black boots. He gathered his meager belongings, including his guns and knives and tobacco, and off they went.

Sam was a plump Black man originally from Boston. He was well dressed with a neckerchief and liked to play the harmonica. He had two brothers who served with General Greene. His sisters and mother were in Rhode Island. He was thirty-two. He was a strong man who carried equipment, pots and pans, rifles, and a walking stick. The journey to Chambers Gate was forty-eight or forty-nine miles. They walked.

"After the war, I want to become a chef."

"A what?" asked Aaron.

"A cook. A chef."

"Aye. Where?"

"New York!"

"What will you cook, Mr. Chef?"

"Pork chops, okra, Brunswick stews. French desserts."

"Great. I will visit."

"There is a spot I have in mind, off State Street docks."

*****

"Wait! Fork in the road. Which way?" Aaron interrupted.

"This way to Chambers Gate, man. They bring in sugar, logwood, and other dyeing woods. Rum, mahogany, and many other luxuries. Perfect spot. Lots of businessmen at State Street docks."

Aaron said, "I was in New York once. I enjoyed it. Lots of water wherever ye look, and high winds. Ships everywhere."

"Aye, Mr. Aaron."

"And pretty women."

"Aye, Mr. Aaron."

"The thing about New York. Too many bloody banks!"

"Aye."

"They spending the money up there. A restaurant like mine would do excellent business, Mr. Aaron."

"I reckon so, Chef Sam. I reckon so. Now let's get closer to the river and look to camp."

"Good idea, sir. We must a walked eleven miles!"

"I reckon so," said Aaron.

*****

Clark, Helms, Bowman, McIntosh, and 166 men made the vigorous march to the outskirts of Fort Pitt. Some of the officers were playing chess as the lowly grunts watered the horses and acted as security.

General Clark said rather casually, "We move those damn Iroquois over the *Ohio River*, and we push them to oblivion, to irrelevance. We take the Forbes Road tomorrow."

"Yes, sir," they said.

"Rook to bishop 4. I want an extra squad on the north bank in the morning."

"Yes, sir."

"Western Pennsylvania, on my watch, is a peaceful haven. For Americans! No infernal scoundrels."

"Yes, sir."

"And maybe a few French, not bad. Can you ever get rid of the damn French? All over the place. Your move, son. Watch your queen…" he said, chuckling.

"Ain't going to see any British, that's for sure. No Tories either. We will kill them."

"Yes, sir."

"Hey, Bowman! Did Kirby and Duncan procure those ferry boats? Watch your queen, Son."

"Yes, sir. Thirteen boats, hopefully four more. Two trips across, sir."

"Very good. Your move. Watch my knight to king, eh?"

"Thank you, sir."

Clark looked at Bowman and Helms, "I want that band of Indians we paid, in the front, on the Forbes Road. Five in the morning. We are paying them very well."

"Yes, sir."

"And that party of negros we saw yesterday. We will hire them to feed the horses and clean the saddles. I want this operation to shine!"

"Yes, sir."

"Watch your queen, Captain."

"Thank you, sir."

"I want a strong rear guard—your best forty-five men. And I want twenty on the wings, both sides. Sharpshooters."

"Yes, sir. Quite right!"

"Checkmate. Victory!" said Clark. A pause. Some in the room clapped their hands. *"Well done. Well done."*

"Dismissed. Go get some rest!" Six men exited the room, leaving the general and captain behind.

"Message for you, sir."

"Thank you, Helms." A pause. "What am I looking at please?"

"Some correspondence and news from France, about four months past, sir..."

"Right." Clark scanned the text by their lanterns. "John Adams...France had agreed to an alliance with the United States on February 6... February! Letters and requests to French foreign minister Vergennes arguing for French naval support in North America. Naval support!" he said to Helms.

"Splendid."

"Good luck," he said with sarcasm.

He's reading: "Doctor Ben Franklin meeting with the court." A pause. "Adams and Franklin extending lines of credit, meetings, balls, letters. Drafting treaties. And Adams and his son go to the opera house. That's nice." A pause. "Sending fresh battalions over the sea. More people."

"More French soldiers!" his captain exclaimed.

"That's fine, Helms. But will someone tell Adams and Franklin—we don't need more men.

"We need money!"

"Quite right, sir. Quite right."

Clark continued reading, but Helms dismissed himself. He walked outside, over a small footbridge. He passed some troops, under some hemlocks, and down a path next to a larder and kitchen and smokehouse. There were several frozen mud puddles, ink black at this late evening. And then he passed a Black man who was smoking under the roof of one of the storehouses. He was from Baltimore. He was Black Potter. Helms tipped his cap and kept going. Black Potter nodded back.

Aaron and Sam had just finished some cooked rabbit and had begun cleaning up. The sun had been down for a couple hours and a chilly winter wind blew through the thickets. Aaron looked over at his pipe and anticipated that sweet earthy and crystal taste in his lungs.

But his attention was drawn to some echoey shouts down by the river. It sounded at first like several people were fighting, but as additional sounds came floating through the thickets, it sounded like utter desperation. Women were screaming. A couple men were yelling. An animal—a horse?—was grunting and shrieking something awful. Sam dropped his utensils and looked over at Aaron. Aaron in a flash began to run toward the river.

With each quick stride, he crunched the twigs and snapped the branches, his head every so often having to duck under an obstacle. Yells, shouts. Echoey screeches through the hemlocks, like torn fabric in a heavy wind. Within minutes he stood at the edge and peered across the frozen Susquehanna, his heartbeat accelerating.

What he beheld was a nightmare. The back end of a massive sleigh was suspended in the air, its front submerged into the icy deep. The horses were shrieking and violently punching with their hooves. And the poor people! Some were on the ice with limbs spread and yelling, while their hapless companions, with drenched hair and slick pale faces, were screaming. Small bursts of steam emanated from the subjects. It sounded to Aaron like a foreign language. Visibility was limited, but he could hear splashes of water and cracks of fractured ice.

Aaron carefully stepped onto the river and ran several yards toward the fray, his mind thinking of possible solutions. People were going to freeze to death and quick action was wanting. Standing two hundred yards from the accident, he heard German cries of "Hilfe! Hilfe!" It was obvious now—if it wasn't before—that these German folks were attempting to cross in their sleigh, and the ice broke under the weight. Fortunately, perhaps, the accident took place a bit closer to Aaron and Sam's shore, and not the opposite one. There was hope to save them.

Aaron and Sam connected at the shore and barked some quick instructions to one another; they looked for tree limbs and branches of a medium thickness. Aaron threw off his coat with the thought that it could be helpful to someone later. They together snapped a strong one right off—seventeen feet, relatively straight, seven or eight inches in diameter—and one behind the other, holding the limb like a cherished prize, ran over the river.

"Hilfe!" Sam heard some cracking as they approached, and they paused. One of the horses stopped stiff in the pool. Two Germans had managed to climb out onto solid safety, but about six or seven people were still swimming for their lives.

Aaron screamed, "Look here! Grab hold!" He dropped the branch at his feet and pushed it toward the victims. "Grab hold! Grab it!" The standing and crouching men turned with surprise and instantly grabbed and moved the branch toward the hole; they squatted or lay down to distribute their weight, and Aaron mimicked this, lying on his chest, arms spread, sliding the branch, making eye contact with the dry folks, and seeing also the terrible and pathetic struggle of the six swimmers in the dark. He slid the branch across the ice and noticed for the first time how fashionably dressed these travelers were; this was evidently some kind of ball or wedding. One of the ladies in fact had a beautiful hat with a plume of feathers that was now blowing in the wind. Pieces of ice broke in front of him but he, a mere 120 pounds, felt safe. Sam also was on his chest, pushing the branch and shouting. It seemed everyone was either shouting or screaming, or both, for these several minutes. One man in a fancy cape was yelling and pointing, "Meine Tochter! Meine Tochter!" What appeared to be violin cases and small trunks floated in the icy water.

The sleigh sank into the depths, and both horses died a miserable death. And others, their veins frozen, their hearts stiffened to stone, their mouths agape, died. A pretty lass in a wedding dress managed to climb out onto the solid blocks, as too did some drenched relatives. Her dress was the same pleasant color of the snow-covered ice. The groom, in what should have been the happiest day of his life, froze and drowned with the horses. Other well-dressed wedding guests—soaked vests and nice cravats and assumedly nice leather boots, with oh-so-recent smiles and recent laughter washed away forever—joined him in his fate. Aaron and Sam saved four lives with their tree branch; after a quick embrace and fast pleasantries, all survivors hurried away from the devastation and struggled back to Aaron and Sam's camp. Their camp had a fire, and that fire right now was the most important thing in the world.

Aaron, Sam, and eleven others climbed up to safety—several unsurprisingly crying and in shock; one lady was clutching her baby boy. But the fact was, Aaron would later learn, five people perished—four Germans and one Irishman. Luckily, the fire from before was still strong. Sam and another man stoked it with dry sapling, and the flames roared upward to five feet. They had no blankets whatsoever, but the folks who had stayed dry gave their heavy clothes to the wet and shivering victims. Aaron distributed some tea and tobacco to those in want. They were grateful, of course, but had no energy to show it at this exact time. The baby stopped crying and fell into a nice slumber. Many blue faces that night stared at the flames in silence and in pain; occasionally someone would utter something in German, but it would go unanswered.

This incident introduced him to Henry McCall, who lived nearby. Sometime after midnight, this man approached Aaron, who was still amped up with adrenaline and felt not like sleeping.

"That was a brave thing you did. Both of you."

"I was in the area, and we had to do…something. We heard it all from our camp."

"You boys soldiers?"

"Formerly, yes. We're going to Canada."

"Why?"

"Get away from the war, get away. And when things settle down, come back." Aaron looked wooden and shocked; he wasn't making any eye contact.

"Where?"

"Maybe to New York methinks."

"Do you realize how dangerous it is, going up to Canada? The Indians, the spies, you'll never make it."

"I can make it."

"Suit yourself, soldier. You have a name?"

Aaron.

"Henry McCall."

"Pleasure, sir."

"If you need a place to recuperate, I have a farm just a couple miles over that ridge."

"I may take you up on that. Thank you, Mr. McCall."

"Oh, call me Henry. Boy that was some heroic feat out there. You saved...four lives."

"I was in the area, and we had to do it."

"We can get it in the local papers, if you deem that wise and prudent, boy."

"No. Let's not, sir." For the first time, Aaron looked at McCall eye to eye with a cool resolution.

"Understood." He paused. "Four lives. Well done. That was a wedding party, they came over from Berwick. Friends of Evan Owen. Do you know him?"

"No."

"Well, I was speaking with Owen and the bride's father. It's ashamed she lost the groom, and they are upset, for several reasons."

"Yes?"

"Soldier, they are upset that they cannot marry off their daughter now, and if you are...available...perhaps I could arrange an introduction?"

"No."

"Understood."

"Thank you, Henry." Aaron stepped away but appreciated the chat with Henry. The man was pushing sixty, grayish hair, medium height, seemed honest and forthright. He was also well dressed, as a part of the wedding party that crashed into the river, so he looked like a regal, upstanding fellow as well. Perhaps staying at his farm was the best prospect. The only real prospect? Roof over our heads, hot food. Maybe some work. Not sure where exactly this was, of course. Things were dead silent that night.

*****

Aaron stood quietly in the dark, looking at the fractured river, smoking his tobacco. He was motionless for several minutes. His thin, lanky frame was silhouetted black against the frosty white river. An occasional gust would lift up his dark ponytail like a little banner atop a ship mast. The river looked like a badly cracked stained-glass window at the old meeting house. For a moment, he thought of Somerset and his mother—her face, her smile, and her strength...

Sam walked over.

"Hello, Aaron. Are you well?"

"Yes, I am fine, Sam. Thank you."

They clasped hands in a warm male bonding.

"Sam."

"Yes, sir?"

"I am done marching for a time. I will take a rest at this gentleman's estate. You are free to do what you wish. I will of course pay you your full fare, but let us not go to Chambers Gate. Not now."

"Are you certain? That is fine with me, Aaron," said Sam.

"You can get to New York and open that eating house," Aaron quipped. That night, good as his word, he put in Sam's palm eighteen British shillings.

"Aaron, our contract was for just *fourteen shillings*, man."

"Aye. The surplus is my...contribution...for your new eating house. Good luck, Sam."

"Obliged, friend," answered Sam.

By the next morning, after a hard, cold night, the Susquehanna was rock hard, smooth as a board, so that nobody save for the survivors would ever know there was an accident on the river. Just as the Biblical sandstorm had swallowed up an ancient village in Egypt.

CHAPTER 11

His businesses were situated almost precisely in the center of the state, perhaps 130 miles from the Jersey border, and 130 miles out west to Indian country. Henry McCall was a wise and important man in this region. He founded and administered McCall's Dam, he had a huge profiting farm and mill operation, and he also ran a tavern for travelers on their way to Allentown or Harrisburg, or up to the lake. This war delivered heavy foot traffic from each direction. Though many people suffered, McCall's was making strong profit, for two years plus.

Situated on high elevation among rolling hills and sharp gullies, it stayed relatively dry after a day's rain. The tavern was red brick with ten windows and the front door facing south, six windows on both sides, and four little chimneys symmetrically above. Around all the windows was sharp white trim and black shutters. The big kitchen was in the rear. It was known as McCall's Tavern, just up the lane from McCall's Dam. His servants and laborers (including Aaron) slept along the lane in rickety and rough outbuildings and sheds.

There were hundreds of apple trees up and down the lane, and he also grew cherry trees and apricots, with mixed success, in the side yard. There was a springhouse and sawmill and miller's house. There were fields of wheat on the opposite field, which sloped down toward the stream. The mill was constructed of heavy stone, thirty inches thick, and oak and pine made up the bulk of the framing and stairs. Hundreds of barrels of flour were produced every month. His regular clientele numbered between ten and twelve local farmers.

Aaron stayed a few weeks, then a few weeks more, and then decided to stay and work. He wanted to work. Anything was better than humping for weeks and weeks through the wet forest, coughing and feverish, like a vagabond. He enjoyed having McCall as a boss. And McCall valued a kid like Aaron.

"With all the money you're paying me, I will be in Canada in no time!" Aaron joked.

"Stay in America. America is the future."

"What?"

"The British ain't going to last here, soon they will leave."

"But in the meantime?"

"There's nothing in Canada!" McCall said, waving his hand.

Aaron countered, "I have friends up there, neighbors from Somerset. I won't be chased, penned up, thrown in prison. There's too much hatred and drama here. Everyone is divided."

"They're all sailing to England. They envy you, soldier. You. In America."

"Going west makes no sense. I miss the civilization back east, and you want me to stray away from it! In the east, you can go to the theater or ball, and eat at a dining establishment, and buy a new jacket and wig."

What are you reading?

"*Joseph Andrews* by Henry Fielding."

McCall took it, opened it to some liner notes. "…employer, Lady Booby, and her servant, Slipslop?"

"It's not bad," said Aaron, trying to defend it. McCall smiled.

"Let me know how it turns out. Say, how is work?"

"Great, Henry."

"If you are going to survive in this world, son, you need to ply a trade. Now I have been noticing you have a love of woodworking, making trinkets and such. I can get you some better tools and get you on your way as a cabinet maker or furniture maker. How does that sound?"

"Much obliged, sir."

"Tomorrow I will introduce you to one of my own. He's a good man. He can take a piece of walnut tree and carve you a banister that's smooth as a dam pond!"

"Much obliged, sir."

"Once you have your trade, you need to go to Chambers Gate and head west, wait out the war."

Aaron was not convinced. "*West?* No, sir. I must get to Canada. And then back to Philadelphia to my future wife."

"You're so young. Philadelphia has been around for what—one hundred years? Go out and take some land for your own, soldier. Put some roots down."

"But the British will win. It's safe."

"Maybe they win, maybe not. Go west. You'll thank me!"

"Sir?"

"You will have a head start. In a few years, trust me, thousands of your kind will be stumbling through here, off to the Ohio Valley."

"Perhaps so."

"It's mighty difficult making my case to you *Jersey* boys! Set in your ways, aren't ye?"

Aaron laughed. "You should've seen my brother. Couldn't get a word in!"

"How old are ye, Aaron?"

"Twenty-one."

"Aye. When you are, say sixty-one, you know what then?"

"What, Nostradamus?"

"America will be filled with *Americans* out to the Mississippi River. Corn and wheat and oats everywhere, my man. And magnificent rivers!"

"We'll see," said Aaron

"And guess what? Demand for good woodworkers and carpenters will be sky high!"

"Perhaps so," Aaron said.

Most days were filled with hard labor and focused concentration: felling trees, shaping them, helping the sawyers split them all the way across—some of them fifty-five feet. These were tulip poplars and some white oak, mostly. His fingers stunk like linseed oil. His frame grew quite muscular and stayed consistently thin. In the afternoons, he continued to learn the fine arts of woodworking and woodcraft. He would repair, sand, and varnish sturdy pine floorboards. He learned the dovetail joint. Soon he was working on chairs and desks. He acquired and maintained new tools. He was looking at pictures and drawings of Chippendale furniture styles—Thomas Chippendale of course was in vogue on both sides of the ocean.

In the evenings, he and the boys could drop in at the tavern and socialize, next to the enormous fire, not far from the cast-iron fireback and grate. Chewing on some jerky or sipping some soup. The highlight was listening to the loud, high-pitched singing of a heavyset German lady with a large bosom and ruddy cheeks. She dropped in three or four evenings a week. A typical journal entry during these months was...*the German lady serenaded us with her songs, much admired but not understood.*

Mr. McCall would feed her dinner and pay her about five shillings for her efforts. She came back several nights a week, would sing by the bar for hours, fat cheeks, bursting smile. And well fed. Sometimes drunk customers would throw apples or chicken bones at her and scream out to "Speak English!" but more often than not, customers would lean back and admire the beautiful and wonderful high notes. The lady could hit a great note and hold, for seven long seconds, like a bugle in the key of C.

After several shows many weeks over, Aaron began to recognize that the lady was repeating some of her popular numbers. Aaron approached an attractive lady by the bar. "Do you know what she is saying, in English?"

"Yes. To wander is the miller's joy, to wander, 'would be a bad miller who'd never think of wandering. Wandering." He paused. "We learned it from the water. The water. Oh wandering, like water, is my joy. Master and mistress." He paused. "Let me leave in peace. And wander! Das Wandern ist des Mullers Lust, das Wandern..."

Wonderful!

"A German folk song. She sings it almost every night."

"Yes, it's familiar. Thank you. Das Wandern is the—"

"Das Wandern ist des Mullers Lust, das Wandern..." she repeated for him.

McCall had a huge Dutch oven and swinging crane with iron kettle; his staff could easily feed twenty-five travelers at a time. Mr. McCall would charge travelers at the tavern two silver dollars per week for board and room.

Breakfast was bread and milk, boiled Indian corn and fresh berries. Dinner was served at 2:00 p.m. Light supper at eight. Most people were kicked out by midnight each night.

We ate boiled rice, salt, and butter. And we eat salt pork with ship biscuit. They will be cooking all week, trout. Veal. Pork.

*****

On the occasional off day, Aaron could take a six-mile ride around the countryside on one of Mr. McCall's horses and soak up the sun and wind. There were many Lutheran churches in this region. He saw an advertisement in one of the villages for a performance for *The Recruiting Officer* play. And a live reading of *Henry IV* at the little county theater.

His body was getting stronger, and his hair was getting longer. It was October 1779. The trees danced in flaming scarlets and golds. Aaron took a few shots with his rifle at the waterfowl and fished for trout. He described, in his journal, the *Cock pheasants in the hedgerow that were Rustling the leaves of the big scrub oaks...*

For hours, at a steady clip-clop, he looked out among the beautiful fields of wheat, rye, oats, and barley. The hardy Pennsylvania Limestone that cut through the earth emitted a stench. The horses could smell it, not unlike a sulfur. The limestone embedded deep into the turf, a tibia bone inside the thick healthy leg. The Taconic orogeny, a mountain building period 440 million years ago, affected most of New England. During metamorphism that occurred during this mountain-building process, the limestone recrystallized into marble, and as a result the limestone and dolomites were abundant.

These Pennsylvania farmers were so sure of the Lord's bounty that their barn roofs extended to the heavens in a show of thanks. Aaron admired their different architectural features and professional roofs. Squirrels, sheep, goats, and horses smiled along every turn. The open blue sky seemed to run forever. The crisp air did good for his health and mindfulness. It seemed he was out of doors about seventeen hours a day; his face was a deep bronze hue. Eventually he even met a buddy, at a local iron works, past the blast furnace.

Mason, the blacksmith, was always there, working, banging, clanging, little yellow sparks sinking off the side of the steel anvil.

He would tip his hat and chat with the blacksmith, who made horseshoes, shovels, hoes, and nails. Also, for recreation, he and Mason would go out and shoot ducks.

"You fought with the Fourth Pennsylvania, and you didn't see any action?" Mason said.

"No, I was much skinnier then. You?"

"Never served. My parents were both pacifists."

"I see. For a pacifist, you sure kill the hell out of those ducks!"

"Ha. Dam right, Abbott. I have to teach you Jersey boys how to shoot."

"Say, Do you like books? I have some great books—brought from Philadelphia," Aaron said.

"No, I don't know how to read," Aaron said.

"Really?"

"Yah. When I was about six or seven, they tried to teach me some arithmetic and how to read dem books, but I wasn't a very good student! Shit. I ain't gonna be a lawyer or writer, I said! What's the use?"

"Oh. Well, one day you should start. Lots of information out there, stories. Drama. There's the Bible," Aaron said.

"I reckon."

"You could read more about blacksmithing."

"I make shovels, hoes, and nails all day. Don't got to read for that!"

"I reckon," Aaron said. "So you never have to read an order request, an invoice?"

"No, brother. I ask them, tell me what you want, and I'll make it for ye!"

"Good. Smoke?" Aaron offered.

"Yah!" He spit out some seeds he was chewing on. They had a smoke together and looked at the barnyard animals on the other side of the road.

"Cheers."

Mason started coughing. "Wow, what is this shit?"

"You like it? Hey, I gotta teach you Pennsylvania boys how to smoke a bit!"

"Ha. We going duck hunting tomorrow?"

"Yes, sir!" They smoked for several minutes and then admired the geese cruising over the surface of the lake.

"Is that your paper? May I?" Aaron asked.

"Go ahead. I can't bloody read it."

"Finally, some fresh news." He read, "The American ship *Bonhomme Richard*, commanded by John Paul Jones, engaged the British ship *Serapis*."

Aaron read the whole two-page story, front and back. "Unbelievable. *American* seamen? Jones? How discouraging. Where do they find these traitors? The *Bonhomme Richard* sinks, but..." He kept on reading, reading. "The Americans board the *Serapis* and other vessels and are victorious. Like animals! Nothing to lose...victory or death with these barbarians... The British population has become afraid of this man, Jones, who they deem a pirate."

"Damn this war. Damn the Americans with this—this—magic wild ride. What is happening?" He threw down the paper. Aaron said goodbye and got up.

Mason said, "Abbott, take ye a handful of dem nails. Just made."

"Thanks, Mason."

He walked down the lane, and back on the country road. He had a brief snack at a fork in the road where someone built a wooden bench. He chewed and thought about John Paul Jones. Pirate.

After an hour of walking, he spotted some kids out gathering chestnuts and standing in a meadow, throwing stones at squirrels. They were giggling with a carefree air. Aaron was coming back from his fine noon dinner; his rifle was propped on his shoulder, and he was looking down in the valley below. The maples and hemlocks and green brush ran thick on all sides. He couldn't see the streams, but he could hear them. Mostly he heard the giggles from the boys up ahead. When the squirrels ran for the forest, the bravest boys ran after them, throwing rocks. The rocks and pebbles flew in all directions. Aaron turned a corner. More rocks. And then, like a bad dream, a monster brown bison stepped from the brush and looked at the boys and got plunked between the eyes with one of the rocks. It roared in anger and broke into a sprint and dashed by the young rock throwers and had its eyes fixed on their younger brother, age six, standing alone in the road. The bison was 1,700 pounds and stomping the turf at a mighty gallop. Aaron stopped and watched the bison in fascination. But he heard the older boys screaming "HENRY, RUN! HENRY, WATCH OUT!"

The six-year-old froze in shock, doing nothing, muscles quivering. He had about 250 feet to live.

"HENRY, RUN!" the young voices echoed through the trees and across the meadow. The bison charged.

Aaron ran up a small mound, unhitched his long gun, bent down to one knee, and focused his trained eye carefully over the smooth barrel. Steady. He pointed just a few inches to the front of the beast; the timing would be perfect...

The boy was frozen. The bison sprinted ahead at 30 mph, like a horse. "HENRY, RUN!" Puffs of dust floated in a line behind the swift creature. Aaron steadied his great gun. The other boys stood and faced utter tragedy. Five seconds. The boy, the gun, the beast, the others, and the squirrels...

Bang! went the rifle.

The boy closed his eyes, and Aaron peered out over the smoke to assess the situation. The bullet sailed high and missed its mark, but it nonetheless had a positive affect! The bison, startled by the sound, slowed himself and stopped to look at Aaron. And he calmly walked away in a different direction, still panting heavily. The boy's life was saved. Aaron quickly reloaded. Apparently, the large crack startled the animal, and it wandered off to look for something else to do. The boys were able to reconnect and usher the boy back to safety. They were just as surprised as the bison was, the crack of the rifle and the mysterious man over on the hill, with a red kerchief around his neck. They never thanked Aaron, but Abbott didn't mind—it was a traumatic situation, and everybody wanted to simply go home.

Aaron was thankful he heeded his brother's advice, RIP—make sure, when out on a walk, your gun is never, never unloaded. Never. And it saved that boy's life. *Thank you, Jacob.*

It grew colder, and Mr. McCall allowed some of the boys to sleep in the garret in the cold November winds. The turkey buzzards, perched on the stone walls and fences, were the only things that cared little for the drop in temperatures. They waited for the lucky day when they could prey on a wounded bunny on the side of the road, or a mangled squirrel. All the while Aaron over many weeks mastered the two-pound clumsy hand ax and the standard hatchet. He made a handsome and precise bedframe out of felled maple.

This was late 1779. News of the war was spotty. Washington and Clinton around New York stared at each other in a stone-cold stalemate and the Deep South, it appeared, saw most of the combat. The Americans had Lighthorse Harry Lee and Greene and others. Excellent horsemen with not much experience with all things military.

It took about six or eight months for Aaron's heartache for Jane to finally fade. By the eighth month he decided to stop writing to her. By his count, he had sent twenty-two letters back east. His instructions had been clear, that she could send back a response to the village post at Sunbury. Nothing. Maybe she was back in England? Maybe she was in New York with most of the other British subjects. Impossible to know. All he could control was his day-to-day existence, his diet, outlook, attitude, his craft and work, his faith, his health. He continued to split wood, work the forge, kept a detailed journal.

He became learned at cabinetry making and the art of woodworking. The softwoods, the hardwoods, how to avoid the knots. He stood at a strong 130 pounds. Five nine tall. Smooth face. Great appetite. A year ago, he was a dead man; now he was thriving. Any time he could get away, he would hunt, fish, and trap. One Saturday he caught three fat beavers down at the creek. He read his Bible and carved new little instruments and toys from wood scraps. He sometimes would think about Jacob, or his sisters in England.

But mostly he thought about food. With his pistol he could kill goose for breakfast and possum, which were plentiful. He slid his silvery blade right across the possum's belly, just like his brother taught him. He cooked it with flour, black pepper, and thyme; it tasted like a pig.

*****

General Sullivan looked at Major Bowman, Captain Helms, Captain Clark, and Colonel Crawford, the big talker. They were at Fort Pitt at the banks of three magnificent rivers, the Monongahela and Allegheny, which fed the *Ohio*. They were at banquet tables draped with animal skins. Drinking beer and wine. Eating venison and goose and wild berries. Toasts, laughter. The Indians raised their glasses. Toasts and grins. White Eyes, *Captain Pipe* (Hopocan), and John Kill Buck (Gelelemend) sat front and center. Toasts and grins.

"Congratulations, gentlemen!"

"Congratulations."

Bowman leaned over to Helms: "Pennsylvania is now cleared of any impediments. No resistance, Helms. We can march all through the Delaware country."

"All the way to bloody Detroit!" Crawford yelled.

"Indeed," they said.

"Aye!" they said.

"We are winning this war in the west, and we will win the war, total."

"Yes, we will!" they hollered.

"And General Sullivan will get his medal." Laughter all around.

"Yes, sir."

"Do you know what this means?" Bowman asked, drunkenly.

"Sir?"

"The whole next generation can march from one end of the state to the other, with no resistance from savages. The future is here."

"Yes, sir."

"America! First time in 140 years! Sometimes it takes a war."

Helms said, "Sometimes it takes a war, sir."

"Let's have a drink with White Eyes and John Kill Buck!" Crawford shouted.

Helms said, "No—that is John Kill there, and that is White Eyes."

"Oh, right…"

"Watch out for these Indians, they sure know how to party! Look at that red furry vest that one is wearing." Laughter all around.

"John Kill Buck, I am Crawford. Nice to accomplish this business with you!"

The chief was a tall, handsome man with proud angled epaulettes on his gray coat, in his late thirties. He had a smooth, deeply tanned face. He said, "Yes, Crawford. We have heard of you. You marched with Braddock?"

"Yes, sir."

"Your reputation precedes you. Nice to meet you, sir."

"Likewise. Do you have a family, John Kill Buck?"

"Yes. A wife and many children. We live on the east bank of the Tuscarawas."

"Very good. Give your family my best! Will you have a drink with me, friend?"

"Yes." They poured drinks and clinked glasses and smiled.

"Congratulations!" said Crawford.

"Congratulations," said John Kill Buck.

"To Pennsylvania!"

"To Pennsylvania!"

And then they brought out the fiddles and the brandy and champagne. They played horseshoes with the Indians. Also called quoits. Drinking, dancing, singing, horseshoes.

"To Pennsylvania!"

"Are you going back, Colonel?" said Bowman, visibly drunk.

"Hell no! Going to build some American forts out here, go to Ohio country all the way to Detroit and *kill* every damn red coat I see! Yahhhhh!" Laughter all around.

"Yes, sir!"

"And if I run into any trouble, my friend John Kill Buck here will protect me!" Crawford attempted to hug the Indian, but the unsmiling chief wanted no part in this, backing away.

"This is only the beginning, Bowman," Crawford continued. "The Delaware savages are on our side, my man."

He saw Helms again and said, "Here's to the Treaty of Fort Pitt!" Colonel Crawford shouted.

"To Fort Pitt!" They clinked glasses and drank, like soldiers.

The men partied deep into the night until it got chilly and they continued, several hours more, until the pink sun made an appearance on the horizon, and the beavers kerplunked in the streams and went to work. The birds fanned out across the sky, and some local farmers and artisans lit their stoves to make black tea; men began sharpening their broadaxes and tools with some flint, and soon the light hit the hundreds of majestic hemlocks, which interlocked and posed like a family portrait. The wind was blowing. The deer slept; the squirrels sprinted down the trunks. The bell in one of the churches started to ring, the horses were set out to graze, and a new day at Fort Pitt had begun. The sun was still low in the sky. John Kill Buck saddled up, climbed onto his mare, and slowly rode out of camp, heading west alongside the gigantic Ohio River, the hot sun at his back.

Aaron shut his Bible. He went back outside.

For the past several weeks, he was making a canoe. Fourteen feet. It would be a great present to McCall—perhaps for Christmas or whenever the situation presented itself. It would also showcase in plain view the fruits of his labors and training over eleven months, for which Aaron was grateful. He banged and hammered and sanded, a couple hours every evening. The frame was propped up on some wood slats, and it was kept hidden under a tarp lest a curious McCall would walk up and down the lane.

He built a twenty-two-inch-wide pine board for the bottom and finished some spruce and cedar for the planking. He banged and hammered and sanded. His budding knife and fourteen-inch ax were taking their turns making magic. Things were locking into place!

He looked up at an eagle's nest, made of sturdy sticks and branches. It was a beautiful and serene day, with a deep blue sky. For several weeks, unbeknownst to Aaron, the mother up there gazed down on Abbott like a supervisor on the operation. Fierce black eyes, set mouth, erect stature. The thumping, the hammering, the scraping, the glazing, the tapping, the touching up, the sawing, the breaks. The thumping, the breaks. The eagle sat and looked with steely eyes. The hitting, the rubbing and sanding, the calluses. The tapping, another break. The spruce and cedar held secure, smooth finish. Aaron wiped his forehead and stretched his back. The eagle looked down at the canoe, and at this wiry Tory boy, with admiration.

The eagle beheld the transformation—the piles of wood planks and boards, and after seven weeks, a smooth and handsome four-teen-foot canoe that weighed twenty-nine pounds. Aaron painted it navy blue. The majestic bird smiled at the finished product. A satisfied supervisor.

The job was done. The eagle flew away against the wind, over the mill, past the Lutheran church and the wheat, rye, oats, and barley, past Mason's smithy, over the hardy Pennsylvania limestone. Toward the magnificent Susquehanna.

CHAPTER 12

One sunny day a man arrived, dressed like a British officer. He knocked on the door and spoke with Henry McCall.

"Morning."

"Morning. We're looking for Jacob and Aaron Abbott, Tories. Both approximately twenty years of age. Long hair. Served in the Philadelphia area with the Fourth Pennsylvania, British. We believe they are on the run, and we think they came out to these parts."

"Abbott?"

"Yes, Abbott," the officer said.

"Son, you think two boys would escape Philadelphia and come to my farm? One hundred and thirty miles?"

"Sir, we've had witnesses. Not far from here."

"On foot?"

"Yes, sir," the officer said.

"I don't know any Abbott boys."

"We have reason to believe that one of them is dead. So there is at least one Abbott boy."

"So you're looking for someone who *may* be deceased? They call this British intelligence?"

"Sir. We are at war, and I *forbid* you to speak to me that way," the officer snapped.

"Yes, I am sorry. Look, I will keep my eye open for these boys. Only vagabonds that pass through here is farmhands looking for work, or Indians looking for a trade deal."

"You are certain?"

"Certain. Can I offer you a cup of tea?"

"No, thank you."

"Pray—any news from the war?" McCall asked.

The man shifted his weight and stood with pride now. "British forces have taken Georgia and South Carolina. We are encircling the damn rebels, family by family. Every hamlet, every town. Just a matter of time."

"Just a matter of time…" the farmer repeated. He was looking off in the distance, ever so hopeful that the Americans and George Washington could, somehow, triumph! And he was also hoping Aaron would not for any reason wander up to the house. That would sure change things. *Stay put, son.*

"I appreciate your time, Mr.—"

"McCall. Henry McCall. You're welcome, son. Good luck."

The British officer rode along. McCall shut his door.

*****

That very evening, McCall smartly summoned the young Tory up to the house. It was dusk. Aaron suspected nothing, a pleasant look on his young (but smudgy) face.

"You called for me, Mr. McCall?"

"Aaron! Sit down. How are you faring?"

"Just fine, sir. We finished sawing up that poplar this afternoon. Making good progress. Some of the scraps will make great firewood. Plus I can make another brilliant little—"

"Aaron, it's time to go."

"What?"

"Time to go. You are being hunted. There was a man here earlier. These woods are not safe. I will sell you a horse. You will pack your belongings and saddle up, out of here."

"Saddle up?"

"Chambers Gate, methinks, is the best option."

"Right. And then?"

"Maybe Pitts or Hagerstown. Go West."

Aaron shook his head.

"I know what you're going to say, Aaron."

"I can get there. I promised my brother—"

"Maybe at a later date. Not now. Too dangerous," McCall said.

"Dangerous? How many Tories are hiding out in bloody Pitt or Hagerstown?"

"Watch your tone, son. You can do it safely. Between here and Canada are crews of spies and vagabonds and bounty hunters, and soldiers! And *you* are alone! If you were in Philadelphia, I would say yes, set sail up to Halifax! That is safe. But walking through New York, to Ottawa? With bloodthirsty Iroquis and American troops all over the place? You will get slaughtered. Give yourself a fighting chance!"

McCall and Aaron locked hands and looked at each other with a mix of determination and a tinge of sadness.

Aaron said, "I will leave immediately." He swallowed hard.

"Be silent. Don't announce your intentions to any of the staff. It could get them into trouble, you see?"

"Aye."

"And, Aaron, you will need to change your name."

"My name? What's wrong with Abbott?"

"Go!"

Aaron bought a horse from McCall and headed west, toward Chambers Gate. He was going at a healthy trot for two or three hours. He thought seriously about changing his name and starting a new life. Pitt or Hagerstown? Head north, to Canada? He passed some troops in the road, but he remained calm and they did not ask him for papers. He passed some Seneca Indians an hour later, and he had a smoke with them. He tried to confirm with them that this was the right direction toward Chambers Gate, but they knew not what he was speaking of.

The next day he was ambushed by three American bushwhackers, but Aaron killed them (near present-day Williamsport). He shot one in the chest, he stabbed another in the neck, and he wrestled a third for several minutes into submission. He twisted and broke the poor man's arm and held his face down into an ice-cold stream, put a knee into his back, and held tight for thirty seconds, until the man stopped kicking and lay flat, drowned to the death. The suffering man with the knife in his neck groaned for help, losing a lot of blood, and suffered and watched his friend die a watery death. Aaron walked away from the water and saw the man in the mud, on his last breaths.

"Help me, please!"

Aaron wiped his forehead with his sleeve. "A pleasure to meet you, and likewise, your esteemed partners. But I best be off..." He bent down and took some loose money from the dead men's pockets, and their knives and pistols and extra powder.

"Give me your name first, scum..."

"The name is *Aaron Peters*," Aaron said.

The man died an instant later.

Aaron let the corpses retain their keepsakes, clothes and boots, but he took their knives and pistols. These he secured into the saddlebags. He reloaded his weapon and patted his horse to make sure she wasn't too startled. He barely suffered a scratch during the fracas. Aaron Peters. He checked behind him and in front, as his brother would have done. He then checked all their grimy pockets and saw no identification, but one man had a Tioga Hunting Club card. Must be from up by the Tioga River, about two days' march to the north. One of the dead men had his eyes wide open in a creepy manner; Aaron walked over and manually shut both lids with his index and ring finger. He unraveled a dark red scarf from the body, shook it, and threw it around his own neck. It was still warm. He could feel eyes on him—sure enough, the turkey buzzards had assembled in wait. Aaron knew that as soon as he mounted up and walked back to the main trail, the winged beasts would sail down and commence their gruesome feast. Aaron trotted off.

It started to snow, and he fastened tight his new scarf around his neck and lips, and squinted ahead through the icy flakes, steering straight on the trail. His leather boots deflected the cold flakes, and his toes stayed toasty warm. His horse walked through the storm unperturbed.

*****

Jane sat up in bed in her nightgown, talking to one of the doctors. She held on to the cross in her clammy little hand.

143

"How are we feeling today, miss?"

"The morning sun tells me to wake up."

"Did you eat dinner last night?"

"I saw the light last night."

"Do you ever see darkness?"

"No, doctor. I am a bishop. Bishops, you know, have very strong feelings."

"Would you like some breakfast?"

"Yes."

"What comes to your mind when I say the name Molly?"

"Molly. Beautiful brown eyes. We put the dishes away. We laughed and then we hugged. Shut the windows, butterfly."

"Philadelphia?"

"I don't know it."

"North Carolina?"

"I don't know it."

"Mr. Aaron Abbott?"

No answer.

"Jane—do you know Aaron Abbott?"

"I am a bishop. Bishops, you know, have very strong feelings."

"Yes, they do. They do indeed, Jane…" the doctor said, getting discouraged. But then—"

"I still have nightmares. Bishops aren't supposed to have nightmares, but I do."

"Oh! Tell me about a nightmare you are having, child."

"You will get me some zero. The zero will make it right."

The doctor looked at his notes for a few beats and then conferred with another staffer. They whispered and looked at each other. The other told the doctor, in a whisper, that "Zero is the opium…"

"Zero…"

"Yes, that will keep the men away."

"Zero will keep the men away, Jane. Tell me more."

"There were four of them, at the toll house. The parrot sang to me. They ripped off my clothes, and the parrot was laughing at me. He probably had the zero in his pocket!"

"The parrot?" the doctor was in a trance. He inched closer to Jane, on the brink of some major breakthrough...

"Yes."

"What did the men do, Jane?"

"What men?"

"The men who ripped off your clothes."

No answer.

"Jane, Bishop Jane—tell me!" Shouting.

"The parrot told them to do it. To own me. To own me!"

"Yes? Tell me what the parrot said! Did you know these men?" More shouting.

"He said, the men must put me in the ropes and display... To display..." Jane looked exhausted, with tears in her eyes. But then the door slammed open and people came running in.

"Doctor, please come!" A piercing cry from the entrance door.

"Christ, man! Now?" He was startled, dropping his papers.

"*We* have a medical emergency! Quickly please!"

"Jane, I will be back. I'm sorry. I'll be back." He wanted to simultaneously run out the room and also look at his enigmatic patient. The man left, and Jane sat there holding her cross.

"The doctor goes to get the zero." She sighed and then closed her eyes.

*****

Two days later, he and his mare needed rest and water. His horse, for example, was barely able to keep a steady pace; it kept stopping and looking around and stalling. Luckily, Aaron saw a middle-aged Black man carrying some firewood up to a painted shed on a frozen muddy hill.

"Greetings, friend."

"Hello."

"I was wondering if I could get some rest in one of your sheds, mister. Been riding a while..."

"Rest in my shed, eh?"

"Sir," Aaron answered, tipping his cap with courtesy.

"You ain't one of dem tax collectors?

"Ha! No, sir. I am traveling up to Chambers Gate. Just want to get off my feet for a while. Will even give you a few shiny pence for the trouble. And my horse here sure would appreciate it as well…"

"Hmm. I'll tell you what. You can sleep in my shed, and we'll feed you a nice dinner—but you will help me repair my leaky roof?"

"You got a deal, Mr.—"

"Call me Rodney."

"Call me Aaron."

"All right, Aaron, come up to the house in a couple of hours," said the fellow.

"Thank you, sir."

Aaron tied up his trusted horse next to the shed, opened the latch, and walked in. Mostly a hard dirt floor in the middle, and off to one side was lumber fragments and junk. No problem. He brought blankets with him. He would stay dry and cool here, for sure, and it was out of the wind. The building was twelve feet by fifteen feet or so, painted white. One window. It was about three hundred yards from the house. He found a tree stump stool and sat on it, lit his pipe, and looked over his new dwelling as it were. He then gave his horse a bucket of water to drink from. After about an hour, he "brushed his teeth" with powdered charcoal and rosemary using his forefinger. His breath smelled fine—check. He splashed some cold water under his armpits and his face. He patted his blackish gray tricorn and wiped it down. And—wait—cannot go to a dinner without gifts! He dug into his knapsack for toys and knickknacks he made by hand, out of walnut and spruce. He also took a bag of tobacco. He left and shut the door. He gave his horse a firm pat on his warm cheek and then walked up the dark hill toward the lanterns.

Knock, knock.

"Honey, this is that boy I was telling you about. Aaron."

"Hello, Aaron, I am Olivia."

"Pleasure, madam. Sir. Thank you," Aaron responded.

"I do apologize we put you in that dirty little shed. We only have one bedroom up here! And a common area."

"Oh not a problem, Olivia. It's certainly comfortable. It will keep me dry," Aaron said.

"Please have a seat. Taylor, get off the floor and git in here!" she yelled.

"Would you like some tea, young man?"

"Yes, thank you," Aaron said.

Rodney said, "Sit down, boy. Tonight, we having sausage and eggs for dinner."

"Thank you. Wonderful."

"And fresh apple tansey. I got apple trees along that fence line 'dare."

"Splendid."

"What are you doing out here, boy?" Rodney asked.

"I am going to Chambers Gate, trying to get up to Canada. I've had a hard time of it. Need a change of scenery for a while."

"Don't you got a girl?" Olivia asked

Aaron smiled nervously. "Yes and no. She's in Philadelphia."

"You a trapper?"

"You could say that."

"Beaver?"

"Yes. And muskrat," Aaron said, stretching the truth to hide who he really was.

"Well, you *should* go to Canada. Most of dem beaver moved outta here. Right, Livvy?"

"Yes. Taylor, say hello to Mr. Aaron."

In walked a handsome thirteen-year-old teen, holding a wooden toy gun.

"Hello."

"Hello."

"Taylor?" Aaron confirmed.

"Yes, sir."

"Taylor, I made some trinkets I'd like you to have. Back in the Army. You like trinkets?"

"Yes, sir!"

"Thanks, mister!" He gave him a knife and fork and toy cannon made of walnut and hickory. They were beautiful and rustic. And perfectly smooth.

"Wow, trapper! You an artist," Rodney exclaimed.

"Thank you. I dabble. Here and there," Aaron said.

"You was in the Army? American?"

"Well—I'd rather not talk about it."

"Did you fight with General Washington?" the boy asked.

"Taylor, he said he didn't want to talk about it!" the mother barked.

"Yes, America at war!" said the father. "It was looking doubtful for a while but... Well, tell us, Taylor!"

"Taylor knows what's going to happen," they both said to Aaron.

"Oh? Go ahead, boy," Aaron said, curious.

Taylor straightened up, cleared his throat, and began, "George Washington is waiting to fight a major battle, and he will win it. And win the war!"

"Oh?" Aaron said with a wry smile...

"And of course, the British will leave."

Aaron thought a moment, smiling. *I don't see them leaving Detroit, or Canada?*

The boy continued. "And the Americans start a new government for Americans. Only for America, and George Washington will rule the land and keep us safe."

"Washington? Right..." Aaron said, humored.

"The British and the French, and also Indians—they can visit. But it will be America!" the boy said.

"I don't know. We'll see... Washington as a... Julius Caesar, you say?"

"Yes, sir."

"He's got it all figured out, don't he?" the father said.

"So we will just be another nation on the globe, like—say England and France? Hmmmm." Aaron humored the boy.

"It can happen!"

"I don't know."

"Well, England and France had to start somewhere!" the boy said.

"That's true."

They had a lovely cheerful dinner of eggs and sausage and spinach, all heavily sprinkled with salt. And good black tea. They laughed and ate and swapped stories—Rodney and Olivia were originally from Wilmington, free Blacks, who moved out west. Olivia's parents had been slaves in Delaware in the 1740s.

"Tell us about this girl you have, in Philadelphia!" Olivia hollered.

Aaron's face changed. He got quiet, thought about the illness and the bear and the cold rain, the bison and the anguish…the hemlocks and the loneliness. Why didn't he die that night? Why? The dinner table was frosty with silence—he dropped his fork, and it made a noise. But he didn't realize it.

"Sorry. There's not much to say. The war made things…complicated." Aaron felt like he was slipping backward and felt tears welling up, but he was able to fight them—fight—fight. He took a deep breath.

"Oh, it's okay, handsome. You just relax. One more tea?" Olivia said.

"One more tea, please."

"Give us some of that apple tansey, Livvy!" Rodney hollered.

"It's comin'."

"We need to fix that roof tomorrow, trapper."

"Yes, sir. You have a leak?" Aaron discreetly wiped a quick tear and got himself together.

"Missing some slate pieces. Looks terrible," said Rodney.

"There was water coming into the bedroom last week!" the boy offered.

"We don't have a lot of money for extra slate tiles, Aaron…"

"So damn expensive, the war and all…"

Aaron suddenly announced, "You don't need slate. I can fix your roof with some good wood…"

"What?"

"I am a woodworker and joiner. I can fix your roof. Will a wooden roof do?"

The others at the table sat silent. Aaron made a motion with his hands and said "You just relax. You'll have a brand-new roof in two days…it will last twenty-five years."

Olivia brought over the desserts and joined them with a cup of tea.

"Thank you, madam,"

"Yes, sweet boy. Eat up!"

Rodney leaned in. "I don't want to joke about this trapper. It's just a leak. And I don't have a lot of…"

His wife jumped in. "Maybe we just listen to the man, Rodney,"

Aaron said, "All I ask in return is two nights' good sleep in that shed. Good lodgings! I see lots of white pine boards I can use. Good wood, sir."

"Good wood, huh?"

"Yes, sir."

Rodney thought for several seconds. "You've done this before?"

"For the last eleven months, every day."

Rodney slapped the table playfully. "You're hired. Thank you, trapper Aaron."

"Do you like the tansey?" Olivia asked.

"It's delicious. So much flavor!" Aaron said.

"Livvy uses the rose water and cinnamon and ginger," Rodney said proudly.

"And pouring cream and this much sugar." She held out her fingers spaced about three inches wide.

"You were talking about this roof—"

Aaron said, "You won't be disappointed. Do you have about three hundred nails and a hammer, and a level?"

"Yes, sir. I will get you eighty nails from the shop and two hundred more nails tomorrow."

For the next two days, Aaron got down to it. He dragged the scraps of broken pine, and split some fresh white pine with his hatchet, and had some extra pieces shipped in from a neighbor's mill. He climbed up on the roof and worked for hours at a stretch, breaking for a few minutes for a sip of tea and a smoke of the pipe. Thankfully it was done snowing; it was about forty degrees and cloudy. He did the back of the house one day, the front of the house the next, and on an unplanned third day he fixed their sides and tough angles and spent a couple hours in "finishing." In some patches he laid out spruce, balsam fir, ash quite thick. He made it roughly the same grayish-silvery color. The shingles were about three feet wide and sixteen inches tall, laid out evenly and perfectly, airtight, and professional grade, every inch and crease and crack accounted for. Olivia and Rodney would go out to the yard and look up at this achievement in wonder, the wife with a big smile. Aaron hammered fast, set a new piece, slid, holding, hammer, next piece. Rapid and top-notch excellence! Like in a painting! And Rodney had a nervous smile, fearing that this boy wonder would suddenly charge them an astronomical fee, maybe six or eight pounds sterling, which was perhaps half of the value of the entire house!

Set a new piece, marked, hammer, smooth, hammer, and set a new piece. Aaron's facial muscles and body locked and unmoving. Like a machine. Every few minutes, he would shift his body three feet over, three feet over, three feet over. Every single shingle overlapped with its partner shingle exactly three inches.

At one point on the second day, in the afternoon, a couple local hayseed mechanics came by, hearing the hammering. And they looked up at Aaron, squinting through the bright sun.

"What are you doing there—helping fix that nigger's roof? Don't you know a nigger family live dar?"

Aaron stopped working and thought a few seconds.

"It's funny. I asked the roof if he cared whether or not the owners down below was Black or white, and the roof said he don't care a lick. If it don't care, then I don't care."

"He's fixing *that* roof?" the man wondered...

"Get on out of here, gentlemen. Git!"

"You threatening us?"

"Git out of here and mind your own damn business. Git."

The mechanics rolled their eyes and left. Aaron continued his setting and hammering. And after two and a half days, he climbed down, wiped his forehead, and had a long drink of water with lemons.

"What can I say!" said Rodney.

"Don't say nothin'. I enjoyed it," Aaron said.

"Oh, Aaron, it's like in the picture books we see at the church!" Olivia gushed.

"Ha."

"Thank you, soldier."

"You're welcome. Thank you for the hospitality! I used up nearly all your nails."

"Can I give you some money?" Rodney said.

"No, thank you."

One of his last actions in this neighborhood was to sell his horse to a local farmer; he could walk the three days to Chambers Gate. Besides, he wanted some cash, some medicine, some flour, and a nice black cloak—all of these things he got in the deal.

"I need to get out to Chambers Gate. Goodbye, fine people. Goodbye, boy."

"Goodbye, trapper Aaron," said the young boy.

*****

It would take Aaron about three days' hike to get to Chambers Gate.

His journal entry before he left went like this: *March 1 1780. I think my father would approve of my choices. I love very much my mother and sisters but they are in England. I love my brother Jacob but he is dead. I used to love Jane but it seems she is gone too. I love the Lord. And the promises of tomorrow!*

*****

Aaron passed some Indians in the road, and then he disappeared in the foliage under the hemlocks. He walked deep inside the misty ridges and valleys that cut across the central part of Pennsylvania. This part of the state was like a gigantic, crumpled blanket, before flattening out to the east and west. He had on his person prepared flour, biscuits, some potatoes, three pounds' sugar, lemons and apples, some lard, one pint salt, extra blankets and long ropes, soap, utensils, a tin plate, and a lantern. He walked past new stones and rocks and dense shrubbery and gray moss. Parts of the worn path were rocky and steep. At times he found himself at such an altitude that the osprey and robins were actually *below* him, navigating the deep cuts of the green valleys.

At the end of the first day, Aaron examined some bird eggs and minerals he found near a creek bed. He felt good, and his legs were getting stronger. Turkey buzzards stared down on him from the branches up high as the sky grew dark. He slept.

On the second day he met an Indian and purchased from him a fine canoe. He canoed for the full day, thirteen hours.

Journal: *Don't have much. But an abundant supply of good humor. Caught a 4-pound bass. Saw eels along the narrows. And then 6 or 8 grouse scattered in every direction. Very cold at night. Cooked the bass.*

At night, he spent his time looking at the dead trees, the slippery rocks, and the wild underbrush all over, in all directions. When he wasn't doing that, he was shooting at the pheasants. He was alone, somewhere between Sunbury and Chambers Gate. He was surrounded by gray and dark-green and black plants and trees, so much so that his view up to the glowing moon was obstructed. The next morning at 5:30 a.m. brought more rain. The blackberry bushes were drenched and glistening with happiness. The frogs and birds were thriving in the mist. The woods throbbed with insects' chants.

Last night he was awoken by the sound of panthers rummaging around the pathetic little camp—there were two, maybe three. With utmost silence, he grabbed the loaded pistol from near his hip, and slowly pointed out the opening sliver of the tent and pulled the trigger. The cats broke immediately, and all was safe. In the morning he looked at the fresh set of panther tracks in the cold mud around his tent and near his firepit.

Journal: *A woodpecker is hammering on a dead hemlock. The mists are leaving the tops of the little mountains. Lots of blackberries, which I wash off in the stream.*

After breakfast, he paddled for seven hours.

He saw another panther, which he tried to shoot, but he missed.

That night in his diary, he wrote, *Beautiful like Switzerland, I imagine. Quartz pebbles and sand.*

The hills were green and steep, with huge rocks jutting out all over, like freckles on a boy's face. Tiny streams and brooks cut through the landscape like lines on the palm of Aaron's hand. The temperatures stayed comfortable.

Finally I met other people, on day three. And thank Heavens they spoke English.

"You speak English!" Aaron said.

"Yes, pilgrim. Where are you going?"

"To Chambers Gate."

"Getting close, only eleven more miles."

"Thanks to Jesus." Aaron looked up at the heavens and smiled.

"Ha, getting tired of this here west branch?" The man said.

"I am getting tired of paddling." Pause. "Say, I have seen three or four panthers out here."

"Yes, pilgrim. They are fast ones! Don't bother 'em! They will run away."

"When I get to Chambers Gate, will I meet some fellow travelers like myself?"

"For certain. Forty or fifty population. Also, travelers who stay at the tavern. Canadian priests and such."

"A tavern? Welcome news," Aaron said.

"Aye.'

"Do you want anything to eat?" Aaron said.

"No. Thank you, pilgrim. Do you know anything of the *war*?"

"As far as I know, no peace has been reached. A lot of fighting in the South," Aaron answered.

"The British left Philadelphia?"

"Aye."

"But they have New York?"

"I believe so."

"And the French?"

"Still around, like insects. They won't go away," Aaron said.

"Their fathers fought twenty years ago. Now it's their turn. I suppose," the man said.

"Rochambeau. Lafayette. Others..." Aaron complained to himself.

"What a disaster—the British is going to run out of money, and they are going to lose this war."

"Lose the war? I don't think so stranger!" said Aaron.

"Aye. Best be going. Need to get to Myers farm tonight and sign some papers. Want a smoke?"

"No. Have my pipe, packed. Good luck," Aaron hollered.

"You too."

"Fellow! The name of the tavern in Chambers Gate?" Aaron shouted.

"Aye. Swissdale."

He ditched the canoe and walked for a few hours. Swissdale. Had a nice ring to it. A couple hours later he cornered and killed a thirty-five-inch rattlesnake! He studied its gray and ebony scales. He chopped off the angled head with his tomahawk and secured the gruesome keepsake in a little leather pouch. He took a break, boiled the water.

His journal: *I wash my shirt and pants in the hot water with soap. Stream, mountain, billions of trees. Moisture. Hills. Limestone ridges, slick with moisture. Chipmunks.*

He cast away his garments and bathed himself, naked. Soap in hand. Saw more Indians and said hello.

He boiled some potatoes. He thought he saw some bears, but he wasn't sure. He did see wild turkeys, which he shot and killed for sport. There was a fragrant odor of burning pine on one of the ridges—probably a small Dutch farm. The ants out there were pretty massive. At night he vigorously rubbed his feet with oil he purchased from the Indians. It cooled the skin and felt fantastic. He cleaned his blades and double-checked that his rifle was loaded.

Journal: *I stretched my tent rope between two gigantic sycamore trees. Along the rocky side channels.*

He slept seven hours. By the next day after another hike under the monster trees, he was almost at Chambers Gate.

CHAPTER 13

"And remember what was discussed last month. I don't want Jews or crippled or Spanish, and we must keep the number of Negroes to a minimum." William Andrews spoke to his wife and three friends, at a long oak table, which had a chipped candelabra.

"Agreed."

"We represent the word of Jesus. The Lord's will be done."

"Where should we go next, William?"

"We should go next to Chambers Gate and the hills to the north."

"Will we find young men in those parts?"

"I think so. And young, white, *Christian men.* As long as the war rages, more and more refugees and adventurers will be drifting west. It's inevitable. And we need young, strong men to join us. Hopefully we can get some good wholesome Quakers. We will build up a vibrant Venango."

"Is it dangerous?"

"Might have a run in with a bear or panther. But we'll likely set traps. Aye."

"Bears?"

"You must remember, the animals are smart. Been here a thousand years! The people get the East Coast, and the people get the western edge by Lake Erie..."

Yes, sir?

"But the bears, they get everything in between!"

"Yes, sir."

"We will remain safe because we will work as a team. We will stay loyal to each other, and we need to find *loyal* men. We will build up a vibrant Venango. Because after the war, the region will boom. And we will already have been there. We cash in—"

"Will we have enough supplies and food?"

"Lake Erie will provide, for certain."

"What if we run out of money?"

"Then we trade for it."

William Andrews was the son of a frontiersman, born at Fort Pitt. His father fought and was killed in the French and Indian War. The young boy studied to be a priest, with French-Canadian scholars up and down the Lake Erie settlements. He married a French-Canadian named Marie. For the last two years, they have been recruiting brave men and women to settle out into the civilized west country, north of Fort Pitt and just south of the Lake, off French Creek.

"Did George procure the wagons?"

Yes, Dear.

"Good. We head to Chambers Gate next week."

*****

Last night I studied the moon's crevices and it started to look like spiderwebs. What are you, Friend? A rounded rock hanging in the sky??

As he tucked his journal away, he could see millions of thick healthy trees and smell the sweet Pennsylvania limestone.

He slowly reached for his rifle because he could hear the rustling and shuffling of footsteps not far away. He clutched the gun and waited, his head tucked behind a large tree, small beads of sweat forming on his neck. The footsteps went left, went right. Wooden buckets banging into one another.

Aaron took several steps into the woods and pointed his rifle. "Hey!"

He saw two small boys kneeling in the mud, holding baskets filled with moss, and behind them some adults. They were Indians. Aaron took a few steps forward.

"Ah, how do you do? Collecting sap?"

The female Indians stood and stared at him, probably knew no English.

"Hello?" Aaron said again. Nothing. "Collecting sap?" He made sure his long gun rested unthreateningly on his shoulder. He tried to grin and put everyone at ease.

"What do you want?" a female voice called out.

"Oh! An English speaker. Don't mind me. Just heard some of the young'ns. Walked over to say hello."

"Fine."

"Collecting sap?"

"Yes."

"Aaron Peters."

"Chuc-a-hannok."

"A pleasure, ma'am." This Chuc-a-hannok was a female Cayuga with her party of Cayuga, who came down a few days ago from the New York/Penn border. A tribe of the western New York Oneida. The lady was in her fifties, dark-skinned, with a sleeveless buckskin dress that hung below the knees. She had a striking bear-claw necklace that pressed against her brown neck. All the ladies had thick, long midnight black hair, fastened in braids.

"Lots of good maple trees out here?"

"Lots of them."

"Do you make syrup, then?" Aaron asked.

"No. We make sugar for our breads."

"Sounds delicious. And your home is?"

She said, "Upper Seneca River. Ehh, sir—"

Yes?

"I don't want you to sell any rum to my workers. Many of you pale skins sell the bad liquors."

"Oh. No. I am not selling rum, or anything. No, ma'am."

"Very good. Where are you going?"

"Up to the fort. I come from back east. You ever seen the Atlantic Ocean?"

The lady said nothing; she probably never heard the term. She turned to three of her female companions, also in handsome buckskin dresses, and barked, "*Choc – hesse – hesse – suwatay. Suwatay.*"

"*Hesse Tay,*" one of the ladies answered.

"*Hesse Tay. Su-Tay,*" the main lady, Chuc-a-hannok, confirmed.

"Cayuga Tribe?" Aaron guessed.

"Yes."

"Well, it was very nice to meet you, Ms. Chiic, Ms. chooc…"

"Call me *Swimming Bear*, young man."

"Swimming Bear," he repeated.

One of the ladies said, "Swimming Bear" also, and giggled. Her only words in English she knew…

"The name the pale faces call me. Young man, are you interested in buying some maple sap from us?"

"Maple sap?"

"It's delicious.

"Sure. How much?"

"Give me that rifle of yours."

"No, Swimming Bear."

"The boots?"

"No, ma'am." He dug into his satchel for a moment. "How about these looking glasses and this fork I made out of hickory, for a few ounces of that sap?"

She looked at the little mirrors, and a bright beam of light bounced off the glass and hit her chin. "Sure, man." She turned and said to one of the ladies, "*Oosay Tay fesse fesse. Oosay.*"

"*Fesse, fit,*" they answered her.

"Say, Swimming Bear, have you ever been to Swissdale Tavern?"

"Of course. Just keeping walking along the river's edge. A half day's march." She was pointing.

"Obliged, Swimming Bear." He turned and walked, but then stopped to address the ladies in buckskin hovering around the maples.

"Thank you for the sap!" he hollered, holding up his small pail.

They said nothing in return.

*****

Swissdale Tavern was on the river's edge, in Chambers Gate. It was made of wood siding, had a dozen rooms and lots of large windows overlooking the water; its red roof was cypress shingled. Behind, there was a pen with cows and goats and small barns, and in front there was a colorful garden with a sun dial, octagonal brass sundial with a V-shaped gnomon. The dial face was engraved with five concentric rings. The center featured an eight-point compass rose. A brilliant streak of light squeezed between a cluster of trees and highlighted the front door, which was painted dark green. A number of horses were tied to the hitching posts under a magnificent oak. Aaron heard voices, and laughter emanating from the other side of those thick walls. He stretched his back and quickly dusted himself, tightened his queue holding the long locks, rinsed his tired mouth with cold water, and entered the establishment.

The door slammed. Old men laughing. German farmers, small boys serving drinks, a fat lady at the bar, prostitutes with heavy powder on their cheeks against the wall. A guitar and two violins perched on an empty stage. The smell of corn and butter and cooked rabbit. Aaron ordered a hot tea from one of the blond boys and sat on a Windsor chair by a window. He lit his pipe and crossed his leg. On a chair next to him was the great book in rich black leather, *Heilige Bibel*.

"Good afternoon, sugar. You're handsome!" said one of the ladies with lots of powder.

"Afternoon, miss," Aaron said politely.

"What are *you* doing at Swissdale Tavern? Let me guess—looking to get aroused, get naked, and then roger a beautiful woman like me? I'm Kit. And I'm clean!" She pressed her cheek against his.

"Oh no. Thank you, miss. I just need to relax for a bit…" He backed away.

"Are you sure, sugar? I have my own room, won't charge you for the bed…"

"Yes."

Kit took a step back and looked at this man. "You ever been with a woman?" The boy brought Aaron his tea, steaming hot and smelling delicious.

"Cheers, boy. Well, I have a wife back in Philadelphia. I hope you understand."

"Yes, I understand, pilgrim. But could you buy me a drink? I will pay you back—"

"Well, I—"

Just then a man entered the scene. "Kit, are you bothering this handsome man?"

"No, he and I are old friends. I'll be back, sugar." She left. The man looked at Aaron.

"You mind if I sit down?" William Andrews asked in a deep voice.

"Fine by me."

"Been a long journey?"

"A long journey, aye," Aaron said. He smiled broadly, thinking about the boat ride to Wilmington and Gibson Point.

"Where are you headed, soldier?"

"Nowhere with any certainty, I'm afraid," Aaron said, sipping his tea.

"You look like a young man…open to possibilities?"

"I reckon so," Aaron said.

"Are you a good Christian man?"

"Yes, sir."

"Can I buy you a drink?"

"I don't drink," Aaron said.

"What, pray tell, are you doing at Chambers Gate?"

"Reasons enough. And what, if you beg pardon, is your business here?"

The man set his tankard down and leaned in closer. "This summer we are heading west to Venango, at French Creek. A new settlement!"

"But there are no roads!" Aaron said.

"We'll manage." The man grinned. He took a drink from his tankard, looking at Aaron's eyes.

Aaron stared at the man for several seconds, filled with admiration and incredulity. The man opposite him was about forty, brown eyes, blue vest; he had a few missing teeth and a small scar over one eye, but otherwise a handsome fellow. The fact that he knew Kit by name maybe said something about his character. He may have lived in this town, who knows? But he was persuasive, the way he talked and gestured with his hands. He was…convincing.

"Why Venango?"

"Ripe for settlers, soldier! The population is 160 and growing. The French have relocated up to the lake. And the Indians—the Indians at Venango are all friendly. All the nasty ones were pushed to Ohio country. We need good millers and mechanics out there. Have you learnt a trade?"

"Yes. Carpenter and joiner."

"Lucrative business. You interested?"

"Yes."

"But it will take six or seven weeks, maybe eight weeks."

"I can do it."

"You certain? You look mighty thin, friend."

"I can do it. No problem," Aaron said.

"What's your name?"

"Aaron Peters."

"William Andrews. Pleased to meet you, soldier."

"Pleasure," Aaron said, smiling.

Andrews got up. "Now if you excuse me, I need to pay my landlord a devil of a bill."

For the next two hours, Aaron sat smoking and looking out the window. The sun was setting. Some of the Indians were fishing down below for sunfish and pike. More travelers were coming into Swissdale and requested a plate of cooked rabbit. A clever trio played music in the corner. Canada? Not going to Canada. Jacob was not there to argue. And who knows about Jane. Who knows about anything? Canada. Tories. Safety. Money, security. *My name is Aaron Peters? Indeed.* And Aaron Peters was not going to Canada. Chambers Gate, cooked rabbit. War. Tea, canoes, Indians, slaves. Sickness. *It's time for a new frontier. Canada? No. Why not.* He ate some cornbread. It was dark. Many people had left and there was much more room. Some of the Indians sold their fresh fish to the tavernkeeper; they dangled from thin little ropes. The light of the moon was shimmering off the river, and they lit their lanterns in the front of Swissdale. The boys fed the giant fireplace. Some of the men were drinking whiskey and arguing about a local county court case… *He was chasing the fox across the vacant lot. And Lunde knew this but shot the fox anyway! It was trespass on the case for damages. It was his fox! You bugger.* Drinks spilled on the wood planks, and the dogs sniffed it.

Canada. Venango. Six or seven weeks. Aaron Peters. In the year of our lord 1780. And there goes Kit, getting a new customer. They go upstairs. And where am I going?

"Peters."

"Peters!" Nothing...

"Hello, Peters!" William Andrews shouted.

"Oh, sorry. Yes." Aaron sat up.

"We are meeting at the Presbyterian meeting house Tuesday to plan the expedition. See you there, sir."

"Yes, indeed. Thanks, Mr. Andrews."

An hour later, one of the blond boys cleared some dirty plates and gathered some utensils. Aaron called him over.

"Hey, boy."

Yes, sir?

"Pray—what day is today?" Aaron asked.

*****

Henry McCall was sweeping the lane and picking up some leaves near the cabins down the lane. Most of the seasonal work was finished, and a number of the boys had gone home to be with their families at the holidays. Behind one of the cabins (Aaron's, if I remember?)—a large object sat up on wooden blocks, covered with a large oil cloth. McCall stepped closer to investigate. When he lifted a corner of the cloth, he was taken by the beautiful finish of what lie beneath. A boat. Nay, a canoe! Splendid. He knocked his knuckles against the side and it sounded solid, like a fine house. And there was a letter too, taped to the side.

> *Dear Henry,*
> *I took your sage advice and went WEST, and not north; for now, anyway. Thank you for taking me in and providing great leadership and wisdom*

and a strong roof over my head. You were a great boss to work for. I won't soon forget our many conversations and shared anecdotes. Please accept this canoe as a token of my gratitude. It was built by the giant eagles overhead and the turkey buzzards in the hollow trees in the shrublands. Enjoy it. Paddle like R Crusoe! Meanwhile I am "paddling" to the western part of this very deep and green state. You take good care of yourself and your lovely family and have a great Spring.

Your friend, Aaron ~~Abbott~~ Peters

And apparently, the young man's name changed, by the distinctive mark in his signature line. The man Aaron Abbott was no more. Henry smiled upon this discovery; he took my advice. Good man…

Journal: *May 18, humming birds extracting honey from peach blossom. We ready ourselves for the journey ahead.*

Aaron, Andrews, and the other men of the group got together, pooled their money, and invested smartly in some vital supplies for the upcoming journey. Luckily, the stores at Chambers Gate could provide most of what was needed. They bought fishing tackle, medicines, canvas cloth, and extra linen shirts; also rifle powder, axes and tomahawks, ammunition for sidepieces, pieces of flint, and some large needles for sewing. They purchased dry goods, blocks of salt, and plenty of feed for the animals.

The caravan was a large one. There were twenty-eight pilgrims—five blacks, nine women, eleven white men, three Indians—packed into three Conestoga wagons. Donkeys, horses, and cows walked alongside the train.

They were off. They made about nine miles, and some of the animals needed a break. At a tavern along the way, the large party camped and rested. They filled their canteens and enjoyed hot soup and cleaned their boots with worn rags and good inky polish. Aaron conversed with some locals who were talking by the hearth. They said the British won the war, and the war was over!

"What?" Aaron said.

"Have a drink with me, pilgrim. The war is over! Our problems are over." They slapped Aaron hard on the back and spilled their drinks on the floor. "Yayyy!" they yelled.

"The war is over?" Aaron asked.

"Aye. I was surprised myself. They led Washington out into a trap, he was surrounded, and he surrendered."

"Aye?"

"Aye, finally! They got that rascal George Washington penned up at the Tower of London. Strung up! on trial. Damn traitor!"

There was laughter and rejoicing. Drinking. Everyone seemed thrilled but the news felt heavy, bittersweet.

Aaron quietly said, "That's stupendous news."

The men shot back their whiskeys, and then shot back another. "Order is restored. Colonial government's back and secure. Damn Tories don't got to run like dogs no more!"

They grabbed Aaron's shoulders. "It's like 1775 again, friend."

"This was in the newspapers?" Aaron checked with them.

"Damn the papers! I went hunting with some Germans three days ago, and they told me. They know people, you see?"

"Right. I believe it. British Army and Navy is the best in the damn world," Aaron said with some pride, and also some bittersweet aura. War. Conflict. Rebellion. Over? He then thought of poor Taylor's predictions, and Rodney and Olivia. Well, can't be right all the time, kid.

"Can I have a smoke of that stuff, man?"

"Yes. Enjoy," Aaron said. *The Tories don't got to run like the dogs?* he thought.

*****

The next morning, Aaron encountered several Indians and traded with them—gunpowder and rum for tools and medicine. Erie peoples, their palisades erected on the hills. Aaron and Andrews also traded for good horses. The Erie peoples were friendly. One of the women touched Aaron's smooth cheek with her hand and giggled.

The party left, and they immediately battled cold and rain and wind. Everything was green and wet and heavy and moist. Aaron's hat would hold a tiny puddle of rainwater in the tricorners. After three days, some of the women felt an illness coming on, and the party gave them ginseng and wild onion for colds. These were the very items they got from the Erie fellows.

Crags and rocks, lots of rocks slick with rain were all over the place, everywhere they went. *We followed a Black and still brook to our left. Fallen branches and mossy logs sat in the brook and all over the woods. Everything was wet. Rocky hollow. Crags and trees. Rain. Wind.* The tops of the trees stretched up to a grayish black sky and took the brunt of the heavy rain, so that the troops below got only mildly drenched. They walked and rode for a few more days. The horses struggled in the mud.

Trees and bushes and vegetation greeted them at every turn, over a few more days. Some of the women were coughing and looked weary. Some of the men were quite sore and exhausted.

Journal: *We made about 4 miles and then met with French traders. They were eating some pork by the fire, but instead of a plate, they used the head of a barrel.*

Three more days. They saw a party of Blacks and, later, a Spanish merchant from St. Louis. Aaron traded the Blacks two of his best knives for a huge steaming plate of pork chops marinated with honey garlic and topped with parsley.

After another ten miles, we stopped to rest. It rained off and on throughout the night. The horses were getting soaked. They had about 110 miles to go, Aaron reckoned, to Venango. They were about 40 miles out of Chambers Gate.

The clouds finally thinned and parted, and the party was illuminated under a deep blue sky. This: *We lay in the grove of trees and to dry our clothes by the sun.* The horses ripped apart the grass and weeds. They, like the people, needed food and nourishment. The sun felt invigorating.

What started out originally as twenty-eight travelers was decimated down to twenty-one after three weeks. Two had given up and were headed back to Chambers Gate, and five had died. It was

July 1, 1780. Aaron's body was strong, his feet were warmed up, and he remained incredibly quiet for most of the journey. Steady, even. Tough. Like his leather boots.

We made a canoe and put her into the river. They quickly discovered that it was impossible to maneuver their bulky wagons over the slimy mud and between tight openings in the trees. Firs, spruce, maple, and hemlock abounded everywhere; some were three hundred feet high. It stayed dry for three days.

One of the women committed suicide; she had been complaining of a nagging toothache and intense pain in her jaw. *Our party was down to twenty.* One of the Indians tried to pull up and rape the corpse, but they shot him on the spot, so they were down to nineteen. "A damn set of villains, this tribe of the Iroquois," they muttered. Out here. *They think there is no justice out here? There is justice everywhere. This is the Keystone State.* Andrews barked orders to the group and constantly looked at his tattered map. But even Andrews looked wiped out and irritated every day.

They continued to march and ride, and sometimes canoe, west by north by west, and north. Some of the Indians macheted a clear path for them up ahead. The Blacks were good at catching fish and keeping camp. What else was there to do, but to keep walking? Keep walking. If you quit, then you quit. Aaron picked out thorns of his black coat and would tip his hat so that the rainwater would stream out, falling into the mud.

Some evenings the party lit a large fire and dined on catfish, perch, and walleye. One man had a flute and produced a few tunes. Some of them sang.

> *Wind is thin,*
> *Sun warm,*
> *The earth overflows*
> *With good things.*
> *Spring is purple*
> *Jewelry;*
> *Flowers on the ground,*
> *Green in the forest.*

Quadrupeds shine
And wander. Birds
Nest. On blossoming
Branches they cry joy!

Unfortunately, at week six the donkeys died and—*We left them at the side of the road. We had about eighty-five miles to go. We were getting tired.* Many of them were severely dehydrated. August was fast approaching. In the evenings they played some card games with a few of the Indians, who turned out were quite friendly.

At week seven they lost one of the Negros, and that left them with eighteen. The rain kept coming, sideways. The hemlocks were drenched and droopy. All was turned to mud. At this point the maps were unreliable; they were off the grid. They sweat during the day and shivered all night, as the temperatures fluctuated twenty-five degrees. Someone had brought with him a barometer and would complain, seventy-four at noon, forty-nine at midnight. It was difficult to go west, as they couldn't see the sun through the rain clouds and towering wet trees. Many of them wanted to give up. One of the Indians climbed up one of the trees, about twenty-five feet, and tried to gaze out westward, like he was a lookout in the crow's nest on the heavy seas. He said all he could see was dark gray clouds, more trees, and more rain coming. They argued for several minutes about where the devil they were, and perhaps more important, where they were going. Some of the women were sobbing; they were afraid.

William Andrews called a council with the gentlemen of the party.

"Gentlemen, our stores are running low. We are about out of medicine," he began.

"We have eighteen left of our party, which started at twenty-eight." One of the men started to cry because one of the fatalities was his wife. Our maps up to recently have been helpful, but now we have to admit, we are going off course. Best guess is, we have some sixty miles to go.

"Or seventy," someone hollered.

"Or more."

"*Godamn* rain!" somebody yelled. They threw down their soggy jacket onto the wet ground with a splat. Apparently, many of the party expected dry hard roads, and a straightforward and uncomplicated six-week march, perhaps with clear signage and friendly taverns along the way.

Andrews said, "My first question is, do we slaughter our two cows and preserve the meat to last us to our destination?"

Six of the men said yes. Two said no. Aaron had said yes.

"Do we keep the horses or are they a burden?" All said yes. Keep them.

"The big question, gentlemen, do we discontinue this westward trek, or do we turn south?"

Yes. Many interrupted. "Yes! Yes!"

"No, hear me out! And take the old buffalo path down to Fort Pitt?"

Yes! Six said yes. But Aaron and another said no…

"What? Explain your logic, Peters."

"We can reach it, sixty miles. I believe in these folks. Keep the momentum. They have come so far."

There was silence for several seconds, until—

"Rubbish! Some of our party is starving! We are running out of supplies, Peters!"

"I cannot sit here and watch my wife starve!" one of them yelled.

"We can hunt and fish," Aaron said. "The Negroes have been immensely helpful thus far—"

"I'm sorry, Peters. I say we go to Fort Pitt. You give the Negroes too much damn credit!"

Another said, "I am not going to pin my hopes to the blackie camp hands. They can't even read!"

Yes, yes. Aaron of course was severely outnumbered. He tried a different tactic.

"And how do you know you will make it? Pitt is farther than our Venango destination!"

"Perhaps, but the fort has everything we need—shelter, food, medicine, blankets. Venango has none of these things."

"But—"

"And the path is clear, to Fort Pitt! Unlike this damn journey to Venango. More like a rainforest in bloody South America."

"Venango will have medicine. You said there were two hundred people out there!" Aaron hollered.

Andrews said, "Final vote, gentlemen. Fort Pitt or Venango?"

They yelled out their responses. Six said Fort Pitt, while Aaron voted to continue westward.

"I'm going to Venango," he said calmly. "That was the deal, and I shall not deviate. Respect, gentlemen."

Andrews got increasingly angry at this point. "Stubborn Jersey mule. You are outnumbered. I could pull my pistol on you, Peters. You wouldn't have a chance."

Aaron shifted his weight on his other foot and looked hard at Andrews. The others made a little circle and looked at both men. Andrews' hand inched toward his piece. Aaron was frozen and stone cold, a few raindrops falling off his hat. His lips were straight, his eyes steady. A few unseen birds screamed out into the grayness.

"SHOOT HIM, WILLIAM!" somebody shouted. William flinched, Aaron never moving a muscle. His shiny, silvery piece hung off his belt, fully loaded. Andrews looked at it, and then back up at Aaron's steady eyes.

"Peters…if I don't kill you, somebody else will."

Aaron just stood there, staring at the bully. His eyes didn't twitch. He stood straight.

Williams waved his hand and said, "Enough of this. We go to Fort Pitt. Peters, good luck to you."

"Rogue," someone said.

"Fuck Venango," another said to no one in particular.

It rained. Of the nineteen, eleven of them left. There were eight remaining: two Blacks, two Indians, four white men.

The departed made a nice orderly line down the trail and eventually out of sight. "YOU'LL NEVER MAKE IT!" Somebody yelled. The courageous eight sat down and took a break. Aaron opened his journal.

Aaron wrote down, "*Hard fortune. Hard fortune. Lord help us…*"

*****

170

August 20, the days were getting shorter. It was raining every day. The eight men were making seven or eight miles a day. At night they tried to light a fire. Their boots were in bad need of repair. They felt thinner and undernourished but, overall, not unhealthy. Aaron continued to light up his pipe every night. The men played cards and tried to communicate even though they had little in common. Mostly Aaron and the Canadians could motion with their hands and get their point across—time to hunt, to eat, to sleep, to march. And reset. Aaron shared his tobacco with the Blacks. They talked about their war experiences back east.

Aaron said, "A Tory on the run from New Jersey. The other three whites were from Canada who met Andrews at Chambers Gate. The Indians were Seneca, quiet and hardworking. The two Blacks were from Philadelphia who wanted out of the big city and wanted a new start. They all had one thing in common: they had Venango and French Creek civilization on their minds. Attainable.

After September 1, they still had thirty miles to go. Luckily, they were able to catch lots of fish at a lake. And finally, after what seemed an eternity, they met some locals. Aaron offered to buy one of their hogs, but they declined. They asked about horses, but the price was outrageous.

"You're going to Venango? What are you doing out here? It's thirty miles…"

"I come from Philadelphia," said Aaron.

"Philadelphia?"

"Yes. Walked 280 miles." A couple of the Canadians chuckled. Aaron smiled at the absurdity.

"Good heavens."

"Might you have some tobacco, good man?" Aaron asked.

"Sure. How was the journey?"

"Mud and rain every day."

"Lots of turkey buzzards, and deer."

"And snakes," Aaron and the Canadians complained.

"Sounds right. Welcome to Pennsylvania!" Laughter everywhere. They did an even trade and wrapped up the small talk. One of the men gave Aaron, as a small bonus, a handful of maple candies.

Two days later, they met some Erie Indians who were fishing, a day after that they met a French family on a small farm. They let the men sleep in the barn, and they fed them hot porridge. Sadly, one of the Indians had an accident and drowned in the river. *They were down to seven.* Aaron on this night thoroughly cleaned his boots and tried to repair/fasten a soft wooden sole with tiny metal tacks and the butt end of his tomahawk. He combed his hair and shaved. He also read his Bible for about an hour.

They were fifteen miles out. Aaron felt great. If anything, stronger than at Chambers Gate. The sun baked his shoulders and back— gray blouse, red neck scarf, nice black boots, everything mud splattered and faded by the weather. His hair fell way below his shoulders. He continued to shave every morning. His brother Jacob would be proud. He continued to lead the party in morning prayers every morning. He was becoming an excellent marksman—picking off the turkey buzzards from the branches. And killing lots of mosquitoes. Most importantly, he kept the others focused and on point.

They came to another farm, and they were told Venango was just over yonder, a day's hike. Journal: *The fruit was plentiful, and their hogs are fed on apples, peaches, and chestnuts.*

Aaron kept trying, but horses were difficult to procure. He and the party could notice the thick forests were starting to thin out; there were suddenly more meadows and farms and domesticated animals. They saw their first dog since when they left Chambers Gate.

A few hours later they met a bricklayer by trade, who was in the area from Lake Erie. "Venango was just over yonder."

Cheers.

On the last full day of travel, they battled cold and rain and wind.

At last, they came to a clearing and saw some houses and huts and a crude church, with a sparkling stream about four feet deep, twisting off out of sight.

"Gentlemen, we are here. This is it!"

For once, Aaron let himself smile. Perhaps the first time since Chambers Gate. He exchanged handshakes and back slaps to his fellows.

"Are you sure?"

"We are here."

Isaiah 41:10: Fear thou not, for I am with thee; be not dismayed, for I am thy *God*. I will strengthen thee; yea, I will help thee with the right hand of my righteousness.

The Lord is my strength and my song; he has given me victory. He has given me victory.

One of the Indians laughed and fired his gun into the sky. Again, what started out at a robust twenty-eight now was an exhausted seven. Led by Aaron Peters, the pleasant quiet man from Somerset who liked to smoke. He led them out of the wilderness, and others had followed. This was Venango.

"We are here!"

CHAPTER 14

A steady rain splashed into the small streams and coated the black hills in the western reaches of North Carolina. Far away, a lone wolf sang into the night sky where a half moon was locked up in place.

Jane Canterbury was awoken at 2:00 a.m. by some irritating scraping and squeaking noises along the far wall, facing south, near her only window. Was it a family of rats nesting in the ancient walls? A racoon, perhaps? Jane turned on her side and pulled her blankets over her head and tried to ignore these scraping and light tapping noises. She could also hear the tapping of the rain against the bricks outside.

Suddenly, one of the metal security bars in the window, ten feet off the ground, started to wiggle back and forth. Twisting. Squeaking. Jane shot upright in her bed, holding her blankets, and staring at the window. Loud squeaks and the sound of tiny chunks of plaster falling to Jane's floor. A sturdy rod of metal was dislodged! It was very dark and rainy, and it was difficult to see what was going on. The twenty-four-inch rod disappeared, and it thumped on the wet ground on the other side of the walls. Jane squeezed her blanket...

"Butterfly? Butterfly, are you in there!"

Jane jumped out of bed. "*Molly*! My heavens."

"Ms. Jane, get yourself together and get out here! Surprise."

"Are you standing on a ladder?" Jane called out.

"Yes. Let's go! We can talk later!"

"Yes."

Jane whipped off her nightgown and quickly put on a warm suit of clothes, some strong shoes, threw some water on her face, and grabbed her pack from under the bed. She slid a heavy wooden three-foot stool across the room to the base of the drafty window. She stepped up high and with both arms flung her pack through the window, outside, into the mud. She turned for a moment and took in the room—her desk, her bed, the creamy and sad walls. Those uncomfortable conversations with medical men. She got on her tiptoes, bent her knees, and thrust herself up to the window, wiggled her shoulders and breasts and torso out, under raindrops and into the rain, and saw the trusted outstretched hand of her maid and friend. She maneuvered herself out and onto the ladder, downward, and landed in the mud. She and Molly tightly held each other in the rain with tears of relief sliding down their faces.

"You got my letters!" Jane exclaimed.

"Yes dear," Molly said.

"Thanks to *God*. You are a champion, my dear." She laughed. They hugged again, her chin locked atop Molly's wet shoulder.

"So how was your stay at the prestigious Oak Hollow facility?"

"Well, I need not act like a lunatic any longer. Let's get out of here. What is the plan? Do you have horses?"

"Yes, dear."

"Did you get the money I left for you at the bank?" Jane cupped some clean rainwater in one hand and slicked and "combed" her tangled nest on her pretty face.

"Yes, dear, that was very kind. You misspelled my last name in the bank records, though."

"Oh sorry. I wanted you to work for it."

Jane smartly picked up the mud-splattered, twenty-four-inch piece of metal, looked at Molly, and then hopped back onto the ladder. With some ingenuity, she set the piece in place, albeit rickety. "Do I need to think of everything?"

"It is plenty of capital to get us some transport to England, in style! One-way tickets. Start fresh! Come on!" They quickly tossed the ladder along the east wall, behind some wooden barrels and small crates.

Both ladies jogged away from the hospital, down a muddy embankment, and over to two waiting horses. They climbed on, thumped their heels, and they were off.

*****

The French trapper put down a bucket, grinned, and flashed some yellowish-brown teeth. "Yes, this is Venango."

A group of female Indians walked by the group, carrying nets of freshwater mussels, which smelled to the weary travelers delicious. The fact that they took no notice of Aaron and his band, standing there, made Aaron appreciate and respect this region. They were visitors and the Indians—the Erie tribe—lived here, clear as day. They could not be farther from any violence or combat…

"Are there lodgings available for my party? Winter will be setting in." Aaron looked up at the sky with exhaustion and utter relief.

"The only cabins we have are occupied. But we can assist you in erecting some crude ones on the quick. You have money on your person?"

"Yes."

"You are from?"

"Back east."

"You are heading up to the Lake, yes?"

"No. We are looking to settle these parts."

"To settle! There's very little here, pilgrim. Do you see any farms?"

"We intend to build our…fields of opportunity, if you will."

"Was that *you* firing those guns this morning?"

"As-tu tiré les armes?" He asked the Canadians.

"I'm afraid so. We were just happy, that's all," Aaron said.

"Shooting guns. You good Christian men?"

"Of course."

"Oui, oui. Yes."

"Even dem niggers?" The man pointed.

"All of us, Frenchman. Who else is here at Venango?"

"Well, yes, there are a few dozen English, up French Creek. And German. An Irish. Us French."

"Splendid," Aaron said.

"A diverse town!" one of the Canadians said. The Canadians spoke French with the man for a while.

The Frenchman, whose name was Talon, complained. "But they haven't cultivated much! Mostly, they are building barns and breeding their mares. More horses! Building their churches and schools. You know the British, they want to civilize every region that they happen upon. A couple families I will say have had some luck with their vegetable gardens and some corn. Many of them are sons and daughters of the French Indian conflict soldiers, back in—what—fifty-five?"

"They don't do much! Not like us French, of course."

"Yes?" Aaron listened.

"But we told them, if you want to be farmers, you have to first fell these damn trees."

"Precisely," Aaron agreed.

"You said you have money?" Talon asked.

"I did—but what is that to you, Friend?" Aaron snapped.

Talon said, "Because, if we are to help you settle in, we would expect some…compensation, you understand. This region is run by us, the French—you see?"

"We'll see about that, Frenchman. We will end up helping you…"

"*You* should be paying *us*, monsieur," one of the Canadians snapped.

Talon said, "Fine, we can discuss later! Go build your homes! Welcome."

"Thank you, Mr. Talon," Aaron said.

Aaron Peters and the party—now numbering seven—settled in along French Creek. They were tired of migrating and wanted to put some roots down. Aaron, the three Canadians, one Indian and two Blacks, Caesar and John. A few of them were severely undernourished, and dangerously thin. They all suffered from one malady or another—bloody flux, fever, the pox, gout, starvation, etc. But they all survived, and now settled. In the immediate circumstances, they stayed in some rickety cabins, and all slept ten or eleven hours over each of the next few nights. They were grateful for the roof over their heads and toasty wool blankets.

The town had made its footprint on the west banks of the French Creek. About two blocks of buildings ran east/west, and three blocks ran north/south. The river was two hundred feet across and, often, ten feet deep in the center.

The population was about 210. The Venango area was surrounded with a few small, fledgling farms and stables and livestock barns. The lone blacksmith along the old lane next to the Lutheran Church was doing steady business; soon he would have competitors down the lane.

They would soon build a courthouse and a tavern. There was a French butcher on the other side of French Creek, and also a school. Further back, along the wood, were two forges and a gristmill.

Almost immediately, Aaron helped neighbors build homes and barns and sheds; he helped his fellow travelers who came with him from Chambers Gate. There was a strong bond within those seven men, understandably. Aaron set up as an assistant to a Miller; he lodged with a German family for a few weeks; and he went to church. He met dozens of friendly people. Some of the church choirs sang in German. Some French attendees had trouble keeping up. But most people in the Venango region could understand the king's English.

> *That person is like a tree planted by streams of water,*
> *which yields its fruit in season*
> *and whose leaf does not wither—*
> *whatever they do prospers.*
> *Not so the wicked!*
> *They are like chaff*
> *that the wind blows away.*

Aaron Peters saw not only these things, but he also saw something he hadn't known for months, maybe years—and that was peace. A number of French and Indians, and some Scotch and English, all coexisted with nary a hint of turmoil or conflict. He availed himself to community projects, helped his neighbors where he could. They asked Aaron to help build a bridge. He helped shoe a horse, helped with a barn raising, helped load the wagons to Erie. He joined an Episcopal church and attended almost every week. Soon, he met new friends; they enjoyed a game of whist and smoking their pipes. He even gambled with Talon. It was the quiet but industrious life. He worked at the mill with a German family and made and fixed furniture on the side. For the last several weeks, he was constructing a huge wardrobe in the old Chippendale fashion. As well as pine boxes and crates for storage. As Christmas 1780 approached, he decorated his tiny cabin with holly over the door.

His first trip to Lake Erie left him feeling optimistic and content. This area around Venango had a bright future! With a steady income coming from the mill and with his furniture in tow, he went up to the Lake a second time, and a third. There, for the first time since Philadelphia—or in other words, since 1777—he encountered and shopped for luxury goods: coffee, books, linens, leather boots, fine tobacco, tools, and saddles. He was happy here.

The water was royal blue, and the blurry horizon seemed millions of miles distant. Large ships sat at anchor, and many busy men rowed boats, back and forth, down to the docks, with stacks of beaver pelts, mink, doe meat, fish, and barrels of powder. Iroquois and Erie people grunted their needs, they shook hands, and pointed to pine boxes and other cargo of copper kettles, knives, blades, and cooking utensils. Random dogs usually circled around and barked their hearty approval. Men walked up and down the docks with stacks of papers, barking instructions to the row men. Other Indians walked by with piles of leather hides draped over their shoulders. Some had powder horns around their necks, advertising horses for sale, holding on to the leather straps and reins. The cries of gulls filled the sky and also the sound of enormous ropes and cables being twisted and pulled, with croaking tension.

He soon opened an account there. He built credit. He packaged sassafras flowers, used as a stimulant, as a bargaining tool, as well as killed rabbit, fresh-hewn barrels. Large timbers fetched a premium price for ship building and large structures. Aaron brought some fetching walnut planks that came from huge trees that were twenty-seven feet around, straight. He visited the chandler's shop with balance scales sitting on his counter, selling buttons and thread. He saw carriages there and talked to the drivers. It reminded him of the docks at Philadelphia.

In addition to shopping opportunities and inspiring pink sunsets, going to the lake had another benefit—keeping up with current events. Unlike the thick forests and backwoods of French Creek, the open lake brought fresh news that floated in from the Hudson and St. Lawrence Rivers, news from New York and Boston and Montreal. Aaron discovered that the war was not over. George Washington was not, as the men at the tavern said, a prisoner in London! Hard to believe. What on earth were the British doing, continuing to toy with this ragtag Army, and driving up their debts and draining their treasury? As he kept reading, he understood more clearly—the French with their formidable Navy were "*all in*" for the fight, and no one could fight the English as ferociously as the French. Also a bit noting: "*...a large fleet sailed from New York having about 3000 Tories on board supposed to be bound for South Carolina.*" Elsewhere is: "*Advice is had from General Clinton's headquarters...*" He also read a long article about the Tory Philipse family holdings, which included the Philipse Patent, a 250-square mile tract, that were "*sold at public auction by New York's Commissioners of Forfeitures.*"

On his third visit to the bustling wharves along the frigid lake, he met a businessman named Piper. The conversation went like this:

"I've seen you up here a couple of times. John Piper." He stuck out his hand.

"Aaron Peters."

"Pleasure." They shook.

"Where are you from, Peters?"

"Somerset, the Jerseys."

"Did you make those crates yourself?"

"Yes, sir. I have a small woodshop in Venango."

"Carpenter eh?" Piper asked.

"Oh yes. Wood joiner, carpenter, cabinet and furniture maker. The best in the area!"

"Great. Have you sold any?" Piper asked.

"Yes, some." (This was a slight fib.) "Are there any opportunities to sell my goods up here? Any demand?"

"Yes. Say, Peters, would you be interested in trading your goods for some of our fine imports here from the interior, and Canada? You could make quite a bit of money if you do it right."

"Do you have any representation?"

"No, I represent myself," Aaron said.

After several minutes of this, they decided to sit down at a desk under a tent and get right to it.

"Cornmeal, flour, salt fish, barrel staves, pig iron. Brown sugar, brandy, newspapers, and packs of cards. Aaron Peters to receive 20 percent of said goods, from each fresh shipment to Erie. Peters—in return…" (The man was writing.)

"Will construct and provide, every sixty days"—he continued writing—"white pine shingles, hickory tools, cabinetry of high quality, ladders. Pine chests and knife boxes."

"Yes, sir."

"We will make this contract good for one year." He kept on writing. "Expires December 1781. Yes?"

"I have no objections," Aaron said.

The man Piper affixed his big and proud signature.

"There's one other thing, before I sign."

"Yes, Peters?" Piper said.

"Are those your horses?" Aaron pointed over to a shed behind the tent.

"Yes."

"Give me your finest cream-colored Conestoga workhorse, fifteen hands high, with saddle and accoutrements. I will pick it up next week. And you have a business partner. Deal?"

"Tough trade. Hmmm." He made a face and looked again at the contract.

"Come on, Piper. You're getting the finest pine chests and knife boxes, guaranteed…"

Piper tried to stare down the kid with intimidation and tough experience, but Aaron simply crossed his leg, lit his pipe, and calmly smoked and stared back.

Someone came into the tent and said, "Piper—"

"Not now. Give me five minutes please." And the person stepped out.

"Okay. Here's what I'll do. Conestoga workhorse, fifteen hands high. You pick it and take it. *But* no saddle and accoutrements. Those are hard to come by."

"Fine. Let us sign these papers, Piper."

They signed, shook hands, and had a long smoke. Aaron Peters was now a businessman.

Determined and focused, every day he would bang and hammer away in his little shop, smooth and sand and varnish, and leave a trail of twisted shavings and broken chips strewn about, like remnants of a bad storm. And then every two weeks he would carefully transport the wooden goods up to the lake, where Piper would safeguard them in his warehouse. The distance was about thirty miles. Papers signed and pleasantries exchanged. Piper was a stand-up fellow. Aaron's skill with his boxes grew; as he made more and more, he became so pleased with their quality he began "signing" the undersides, as if they were works of art. He did this with a branding iron that burned into the wood,

A PETERS
PENN.

*****

Aaron spent most evenings sweeping out his shop with the many shavings and chips. It made great kindling for his fire. Every six to eight weeks, Aaron would get his fine goods (described in the contract) loaded up on a wagon and pulled back to Venango. Aaron would procure what he wanted, and he would sell the remainder to the villagers for a suitable sum. He was making good sums of cash, especially for a twenty-one-year-old. Both men trusted each other, and the first year went well. In about three months, Aaron had put away about forty shillings in his iron safe. He also quietly donated a bulk of cash to the new church they were building in Venango, a Presbyterian meeting house, made of both brick and lumber. He also provided sturdy pine shelves for one of the German schools under the huge maple. One of the attractive female teachers gave him tight hugs and cried out, "*Danke! Danke!*" He said hello to the boys and girls who walked to school in the vicinity of his woodshop, and over a couple weeks he learned their names: Samuel, John, Tom, Kitty,

Bernadette, Noelle, and more. The kids provided a bright energy that reminded Aaron of his little sisters.

Aaron had built himself a compact little cabin on the north end of town about three hundred paces to the water's edge. It had one room. Two hundred forty square feet. Secure and airtight fireplace.

For exercise, he walked along the old Brokenstraw Path near Fort LeBouf. There was a Swiss couple who had a house in those parts, and Aaron liked bringing them gifts. They had small children, and he still was good about carving out little toys and spoons and Army figures out of pine, beech, and cherry. They made great birthday gifts!

"Mr. Aaron, you recall our beagle had dem puppies last month."

"Yes, Heller," Aaron said.

"We want you to choose one and take it home with you."

"Really?"

"Yes. Two males, two females remain."

"Thank you!" Aaron said.

They had tea and nibbled on some bread for a while and talked about the weather, local politics, the new church, and Heller's children. Aaron looked at the cute, warm little litter on the blankets in the corner. As he spoke to Heller, he mentally picked out which puppy he wanted to take home.

One of the Heller girls was in the other room singing, "To wander is the miller's joy, to Wander... Das Wandern ist des Mullers Lust, das Wandern..."

Aaron lifted a finger and smiled. "Wait. Yes. I know this. It's about a wandering miller, he wanders all over. A German song!"

"Beautiful, child. Please sing it again!" Aaron said thirty minutes later.

The wiry young businessman kneeled down to one knee. "You, my friend, shall forever be known as... Gulliver." He set the little fellow in a basket.

"Thank you, Heller."

"Aye. See you at church, Peters." The door closed.

*****

The ladies were relaxing at a fancy tavern in New Bern, North Carolina, along the banks of the Neuse River. Molly looked at Jane.

"And they bought it? All of it?"

"Yes. Don't act surprised, woman. I took acting classes! Every student needs to know how to act mad…this whole world has gone mad, I've often said." Jane was well-bathed and made over, with a nice silk dress and black shoes.

"Eat some more bread and soup. You have lost weight."

"Thank you. Can I eat your pork?"

"Yes, help yourself."

"What time does the ship leave?" Jane asked, tearing into her lunch and chewing.

"In about three hours. We'll pay our bill and head out for the docks. Nice day to sail."

"It is a nice day. It's a day…" Jane looked sullen.

"Butterfly, what is the matter? Butterfly?"

"I realize it's been—what—three years. Three and a half—"

"*Please* don't ask me about this dear!" snapped Molly.

"But have you heard anything from Aaron?"

"No, dear. Nothing. Finish that bread up."

"He didn't return to Philadelphia?"

"No."

"Nothing?" Jane demanded.

"Well. Hmm. I will tell you something. Do you promise you will not get too crazy? Because I know you can be crazy—you've proved that!"

"What is it?" A pause. "*Molly!*"

"I got a letter from Ms. Robertson on Vine a couple years ago."

"Peg!"

"Yes, Peg."

"She said when they…cleaned out our house and removed all the furniture and prepped it for sale, she said they found"—she paused—"about twenty handwritten letters from one A.A. to Ms. Jane Canterbury, 380 Vine Street."

"My *god*." She held her face with her hand. "My god. He didn't die. He's alive."

"Perhaps."

"He's alive and he's in Pennsylvania."

"Jane. He could be anywhere. He could be in England even!"

"He's alive. The handsome young courier. The heavens have granted us a miracle. There is a God above, and good gracious, he has left the door open!"

"This was some time ago. We do not know of his well-being today, Jane. Listen! This sounds like you are endeavoring to do something incredibly dangerous, Jane. There's still a war going on. Won't you sail to England with me, get some rest, and then we reassess the situation?"

Jane looked out the window down the lane, at the marina and huge masts. "Ha, it looks like I have only two hours left to decide!"

"I do remind you, I have two tickets in my purse." One of the loud boat horns belched off, for all of New Bern to appreciate.

"He could be anywhere. Canada? Perhaps you are right…" Jane sighed.

"Yes. Quite often I am!"

"I love you, Molly."

"I love you too, Butterfly."

"*My words fly up, my thoughts remain below: words without thoughts never to heaven go.*"

"Is that Shakespeare?" asked Molly.

Jane smiled, and there was an odd silence at the table for half a minute. They looked at each other. "Pay the bill. I will freshen up." She got up, walked over to Molly and stood behind her, held her shoulders, leaned in, and said quietly, "It's decision time."

"Oh dear…"

*****

For Christmas, Aaron decided to have a little party at his cabin; attendees were the Frenchman Talon, his business partner Piper, the Canadians, the Indian, and Caesar and John. Heller also stopped in. They sat around a big table next to a roaring fireplace. Little Gulliver scurried around, sniffing everybody. They drank wine and played whist. Talon brought dessert pudding, and Piper brought a bottle of strong Canadian whiskey. It was a colorful room, seeing that everyone had on their striking attire—navy, light green, brown coats—and caps and hats and cravats. Pipe smoke filled the room, and there was a substantial pile of money in the center.

"Caesar and John are going into commercial fishing," said Aaron. He was holding a big bowl of sauerkraut with dried anchovies.

"Yes, indeed," they said.

Piper said, "Next time you are up at the Lake, look me up, let's talk. Mighty competitive."

Heller said, "You should fish along the banks of the Allegheny. Much better catch."

Someone yelled, "Move your hand, I cannot see the bloody trump card, ye rascal."

"Bugger you!"

"Bugger off!"

"Same suit. You don't have spades?"

"Let him play, Talon."

"We will also look at business opportunities at Fort Pitt."

"Wise move. That area will explode over the next twenty-five years. Ye boys are so young."

"Move your hand." A pause. "You lost. I have a seven."

"It's not your turn, Heller."

"Pour me a drink, Peters."

"It's his turn. Which one is your glass?"

"We go clockwise, you damn Canadian. It's his turn!"

Gulliver started barking, and Aaron gave him some venison to nibble on.

"Ah shit…"

"It's all right. Gulliver will eat that," Aaron said.

"This is good whiskey. No, not that Canadian shit. The local stuff."

"Yes, sir. Piper, you should go into the whiskey business!"

"Whiskey in Pennsylvania? No, thank you."

"Put the trump card faceup, ye cheaters," Caesar said.

"You know what my cousin told me, in France?" asked Talon.

"What, Frenchie?" Heller said.

"They are constructing these...flying balloons, filled with hot air, and you can fly."

"Really? Who is?" the whole table wondered aloud.

"Some French scientists."

"Flying balloons, eh? How much whiskey have you had?"

Laughter all around.

After another hour of this, Heller's daughter came over and started singing. The nine gentlemen loved it and told her to go on. She did another one. And then she started on a relatively new (1760) one, and everybody jumped in and sang loud and enthusiastically, with glasses rolling off the table and breaking, and Gulliver howling his approval.

> God rest ye, merry Gentlemen,
> Let nothing you dismay,
> For Jesus Christ our Savior
> Was born upon this Day.
> To save poor souls from Satan's power,
> Which long time had gone astray.
> Which brings tidings of comfort and joy.[7]

Many of the men had their arms around each other and laughing. "Merry Christmas!"

The Indian jumped up and hung on the crossbeams, suspended lengthwise, that held up Aaron's roof.

"Merry Christmas!" The laughing and shouting and caroling echoed past sleeping horses, over the creek, through the barren forests and shrouded coyote dens, and across icy-cold darkness.

And then in late January it snowed violently and aggressively, and it howled, like the continuous racket when you sit on top of a pipe organ. Didn't let up. The air and the ground and the river and everything were stark white, except the tops of brown chimneys belching out some heat. So much snow, it rose up beyond the tops of barrels, and halfway up people's homes. Snow. Kept coming for nine days. The temperature was locked in at ten or fifteen degrees.

The naked trees stood like large sticks, caked with ice. Snow bunnies would periodically sprint from one set of trees to another. The air smelled like more snow and sweet, dried wood cooking in many a hearth. The villagers fed their animals plenty of hay and feed, and kept the fires lit all night. The snow below was covered with ice, and then plenty of snow, and more snow. Perhaps five feet, from Venango to the lake, and to the west, into Ohio country. Luckily, the main road up the lake (and back) was plowed by sets of oxen.

One winter night in February 1781, he was coming back home from the lake, with his saddlebags filled with fourteen more shillings. Two more feet of snow had fallen. The night air was still like a medieval wall. All was quiet. He secured his horse into the barn and provided plenty of hay. The walls were solid and protected the mare from the fierce winds outside. The beast was smiling to finally be under a dry and solid roof. Aaron started a blazing hot fire and prepared a nice cup of tea. Above his fireplace was a worn yellow flag that said, SOMERSET COUNTY 1688. A big broad ax sat in the corner and a set of keys dangled on a wall hook.

He unfastened a bundle of papers, letters, and bulletins. He read recent (1781) news and dispatches that the *war* was alive and well. Would it ever end? He read about the boy wonder Lafayette, dancing around North Carolina and Virginia like a ghost. Catlike, playful, brash, outnumbered, he hit the flanks of large armies and exhausted them. Aaron shook his head in disbelief. The British with seven thousand men and Lafayette has (reading)...seven hundred men! And the Frenchman hit them and hit them and hit them, in the mouth. As he folded up the news and inhaled from the pipe, he thought, for the first time in his young life, that the Americans had a decent chance of breaking off from England and establishing their own nation. Imagine a cat and mouse, jabbing and hitting and ducking and dancing, for seven years! The advantage now was with the mouse. He would never admit it, but—but—he wouldn't be disappointed if the Americans would win this damn war. The heart and passion. The fight!

Aaron flipped through the icy cold papers, and to his delight—a miracle!—he opened and read a letter from his sister! He set his pipe aside and showed complete focus...

They all arrived safely in England. (Reading.) Sadly, it mentioned to say hello to Jacob for them. She was married to a bookseller and living in Bristol. (Reading.) She celebrated her seventeenth birthday with a delicious cinnamon cake. *Mother says hello. We love you and Jacob. We love you!* (Reading.)

Aaron started to cry but tightened up and fought it off. He was so happy and calm and at ease. His family was safe; the words were in his hands! Mother had found lodgings with a distant relative. The girls were in school. (Reading.) The letter described a visit to Hampton Court Palace and brilliant Tudor gardens. Everyone was healthy, and that was the most important. Even Aaron would never forget he went from a weight of 97 to about 127. Progress. Just like America herself.

He read the letters a second time and smiled. He put his jacket back on and left his blazing fire. He stepped from his cabin into the bracing cold, his black boots crunching into the snow. Most of his neighbors were sleeping. French Creek flowed with silence around cakes of ice. He looked up at the ink-black sky and studied some of his favorite constellations. Gemini, Virgo, Cancer. Yes, that was it. His breath was visible, every few seconds, like an old friend.

And there was the Leo constellation. The great lion, the mane and shoulders and powerful feet. Representing strength and fortitude and determination.

Aaron Peters—twenty-two years old from Somerset, New Jersey, pockmark scars on a handsome face, wearing a thick black cloak and wine-colored scarf, strong and thin, a man who wasn't sure where he would live but knew that he found a home—went back inside his cabin and shut the door.

Gulliver fell fast asleep, and then so did Aaron. It started to snow again.

*****

The *HMS Dolphin* plowed through a rolling greenish-blue sea on a northeast trajectory, producing a cold spray, starboard, and port sides, like little watery wings. There were roughly eighty-five souls onboard; the entire vessel was 112 feet. It bobbed and rocked rather smoothly like a sleeping giant, crashing through large, thick waves of water like they were toothpicks. The canvas sails were stiff and taut. Many travelers were above decks, enjoying some sun and breeze—a mix of families, businessmen, military figures, and clergymen, the majority European-born. Some of them chatted, some of them read, but most simply gazed out along the mysterious horizon and contemplated the wonders of the deep. One traveler—a female from Philadelphia—stood in the sun holding one of the smooth rails with both hands, looking at the tiny whitecaps below her. She was alone and knew no one here, but over the course of four weeks, she would become friendly with several. Her name was Molly Kildare.

*****

March 1781.

A six-year-old North Carolina girl stood up off the grass, set aside her doll, and ran through a brownfield of as-yet blooming sunflowers, toward the road, in her bare feet. You could hear the deep thumping, clanging, and the racket starting from far away and getting louder until it seemed like it was right on top of the world, behind Oak Hollow Lake. There was a loud rhythm to it. Wooden wheels were crunching over tiny rocks. Horses were panting and chanting to one another. Occasionally a man's voice would belt out some command. She stood a safe distance off the road and looked to the left and to the right, and she saw four thousand colonial troops, dressed in a varied assortment of navy, tan, brown, gray, and light blue and with black boots and shiny, sharp weapons glistening in their hands. Here was General Greene and Light Horse Harry Lee, and North Carolina militia, backwoods riflemen, Virginia militia, a dozen six-pound cannons pulled by horses, more Virginia regiments, Delaware infantry, and the First and Second Maryland Regiments. They all looked straight ahead, they marched, they turned in unison, they marched, and slowly they faded out of sight beyond the hills, and the dust and the noise finally abated. And then, after forty exhilarating minutes, the road was empty. The girl walked onto the road and watched the clouds of dust growing fainter. Fainter still. Silence, now, and emptiness on the horizon.

The End

About the Author

Ben grew up in Ohio and studied communications at Allegheny College in Pennsylvania. He played basketball for the Gators, and during warmer months, he enjoyed swimming and hiking at Conneaut Lake and Woodcock Dam, inspired by the many hemlocks (the state tree of Pennsylvania).

He lives and works in Washington, DC. On weekends, he listens to his vinyl record collection and plays and reads with his daughter, Emilie.

Hemlocks is his first book.

CPSIA information can be obtained
at www.ICGtesting.com
Printed in the USA
BVHW071240200921
617096BV00002B/102

9 781662 444241